Everyday Life in the Village

How a series of disasters resulted in happiness
for an English couple on a Greek island

By Michael Saunders

Copyright © Michael Saunders, Athinaika Nea, 2005

Editor: Hilary J Teplitz
Designer: Yannis Smyrnis
Cover design and illustrations: David E Smith

The chapters of this book first appeared in the *Athens News*, Greece's English-language weekly newspaper.

ISBN 960–86395–8–1

Printed and bound in Athens, Greece by Psyllidis Graphic Arts.
Pre-press by Multimedia S.A.

Contents

CHAPTER ONE

Arriving in paradise

We'd bought the house many years before; a concrete block and asbestos roofed affair, set in a tiny mountain village on a Greek island. Over time we modernized it and used it for holidays.

Now we'd reached that age when the sand in our egg timer was ebbing away. Did we have the bottle to realize our dream, or would the runny egg of time become hardboiled, too late in our dotage for us to make the move?

In England everyone had said how brave we were, while behind our back they secretly smirked at our stupidity. Surely only mad fools could contemplate leaving behind the bounty of suburbia, with its four wheel drives, wide screen tellies and all that lawn to mow. Why, there wasn't even a McDonalds on the island or, even worse, one of life's prerequisites, an Indian takeaway - that indispensable essential of modern British life. Neighbours had heard a rumour that meat was actually dead animals. It didn't come in neat little cling-filmed polystyrene trays, with labels and sell by dates. God, we were going back to the dark ages.

The house had obviously taken umbrage over having been left it to its own devices into the winter. It was cold, dark and altogether uninviting. But there we were - sold up lock, stock and barrel. Everything seemed all rather daunting. And then, around eight 'o clock the sun peeped over the mountains above us and our misgivings began to thaw. We set to and by mid-morning had cleared through and were sitting on the terrace basking in the warm January sun.

Frozen suburbia eat your heart out. We were in paradise.

Did we have a cunning plan?

Now that we were actually here, the house appeared to have shrunk. There was a forty foot container languishing back in the UK, full to the gunwales with all our effects. We needed them here to make the house feel more at home - at least that was the reasoning at the time. We were stuck now, and there was no way everything was going to fit. We were going to have to extend. Not one room, but triple the existing house size!

Unknowingly, we were to be lambs to the slaughter, shoved through a maze of bureaucracy designed to gobble up innocents abroad, in a labyrinth that would defy even Theseus!

At first, things went swimmingly. I spent hours drawing plans - and then many more redrawing them, as Pauline decided the bathroom was too small, as was the bedroom, and the new sitting room looked a little cramped too. What began as a small extension was growing by the hour. However, comprises were made - I did as I was told - and the final drawings were completed.

We took them into town to Yiannis, a very rotund *mechanikos*, who waxed lyrical over the unusual design and promised to visit our house the very next day in order to survey the land.

Two weeks later, he arrived! Delving into his briefcase, he produced a tape measure and a piece of paper. With much head turning, puffing and squinting, he drew a rough approximation of the land and the house, before getting down to more serious business. He lounged against the wall, holding the tape measure between two podgy fingers, while I ran around the garden with the other end, to various pertinent points.

"How many pondus you have there, Michali, please?"

"Fifteen metres, twenty," I called out, and he would jot this measurement down before sending me scrambling to the next spot.

With measurements duly taken we were informed everything would be drawn up within the week, ready for a Planning License application.

The week came and went, and another and then one month later, Yiannis arrived, puffing up the garden path, carrying a thick sheaf of papers. Proudly he spread the plans out on the table. The land survey showed our boundaries criss-crossed with a series of ley lines, which were the measurements I had called out. And then we were presented with the piece de resistance - computer generated drawings of our new extension. They bore absolutely no resemblance to our original design. A plan view of dining table and chairs appeared in the bedroom. And what was this - kitchen units in the bathroom? This wasn't our house, was it? In fact, what was originally a single storey had grown another floor!

Yiannis shrugged his shoulders and waved his hand dismissively.

"No problem, Michali. You need two floors. You have better view. See? Imagine waking up with your beautiful wife - there," and he leeringly jabbed a finger at what was supposed to be the bathroom.

"But we only wanted one floor."

"Ah, Michali, Michali. This is only for the Planning License. Maybe you will want two floors in the future. Who can tell?"

Me!

"You don't have to build this house. If you want a bedroom here, or here, it's no problem," and he touched the side of his nose conspiringly. "This is only for planning purposes, *katalaves*?"

I wondered whether he trundled out the same computer generated design for every client. The name of the game appeared to be Planning License. What you built thereafter mattered not a jot - provided the perimeter did not exceed the sanctioned design.

"How long will it take for permission to build?"

He pursed cherubic lips. "Soon. Maybe one month, maybe not," and shrugged his shoulders.

Winter melted away into spring and the sun began to scorch an early summer, new friendships were forged and old ones were renewed - and still we waited.

A rude awakening

"Are you awake?"

I wasn't, but the elbow in my ribs did the trick.

"Listen... there's someone outside. Go and see."

I cocked an ear off the pillow and listened. With a sigh, I swung my legs out of bed, tottered to the window and peered out through a chink in the curtains. Nothing! Stumbling back, mumbling something about a cat, I collapsed onto the bed, only to be resurrected by an urgent hiss in my ear.

"There is someone out there!"

Grumbling, I dragged on my shorts and lurched towards the front door. Sunlight seared through sleep encrusted eyes, and I staggered out into the day. I stood there, eyes closed, spiky hair combed by the pillow and slumber mark creases running down my face. Not a pretty sight!

Desperately focussing bleary eyes, I rapidly awoke on seeing Nikos brutally shaking our new, metal fence for all he was worth. My Greek isn't up to much, but I'm totally fluent in swearing! A string of curses haltered the clattering.

Fencing to separate our garden from his olive grove had been erected between two existing garden walls. This direct line constituted the boundary as marked on our deeds. However, the law is an ass and these deeds were apparently worthless, according to Nikos. He and umpteen predecessors before him had owned this land since time immemorial. Everyone knew that when Dimitris had built the house we lived in - twenty five years ago - he had pinched some land.

Now, it was due for return, he reckoned.

Oh no it wasn't! I stood my ground, pretending not to understand, and Nikos huffed and puffed before gradually running out of steam. He went away in a sulk and stopped speaking to me altogether.

A few days later we had trouble on the other side of our land.

"Michali! *Ela 'tho!*"

Christos leaned threateningly over the new fence, his black moustache quivered with anger, as he demanded to know why we had erected a fence when everyone knew there was a right of way across our garden.

"How do I bring my olives through?"

I took the wind out of his sails. "No problem, just open the fence and come on through."

Apparently the pathway had last been used twenty years ago. But this was a point of principle, and principle is an important part of village culture.

The sacred olive tree

So too is tree surgery. It can land you in hospital or, worse, in clink.

There is a carob tree in the next olive grove, which overhangs one of our windows. I cut back the offending branches to give us more light. OK, so I may have pruned back a little way past the actual boundary line, but what did that matter? It would seem, a lot.

All hell let loose when the owner discovered the surgery. From the torrent of abuse, I gathered he was less than happy. It was his tree, not mine. I had no right.

In fact, I had, because I'd checked after another little contra temp.

I was having coffee when I heard a bang on the door. It was the law! Now what?

"*Ela.*" The policeman waved me outside.

There in the lane stood my arch enemy, Stelios, giving vent

to something I was supposed to have done. The wizened little man always wears a grimace, as if he were sucking a lemon. I have never known why he finds me so offensive, apart from when I cut down a few of his olive branches. How was I to know this was a hanging offence? I said sorry, but Stelios never ever forgave me, and from that time on there has been a vendetta. The policeman motioned me towards Stelios' olive grove.

"Look!" Stelios spread his arms. The policeman and I looked.

There was one roof tile lying on the ground, which Stelios picked up and smashed against a rock. He waved a broken piece under my nose.

"See!"

I didn't understand. When we were having a new roof built, one tile had ended up on his land. Rather than ask me to remove it, he had called in the police. By now I was getting used to official procedures.

"Passport... father name... mother name."

The complaint was duly logged in police files. If I step out of line again, I could go to prison.

And yet, sometimes you just have to risk it. It's called living life to the full - or is it merely stupidity? Across the lane there is a gap between the olive trees, where I park my car. I have used this spot for years and never has there been a problem. However, of late, the olive trees have grown a little denser and when I drive under them, they scratch the roof. They only had a few olives, so I cut off a branch. Well, ok, four, if you want to be picky. Nothing drastic you understand - just small ones. After the operation the car fitted beneath, perfectly. All was well with the world. Except, I upset Stavros - he keeps bees and had promised me a jar of his finest honey. But not now.

He was waiting for me when I parked.

"You cut my olive tree down. It's my olive tree. I'll call the police. You'll go to prison," and he crossed his wrists, as if

they were manacled, to reinforce his argument.

I decided it would be foolish to complain, or point out it was a slight exaggeration to say I had actually cut the olive tree down. I know you can't touch another man's olive tree, but hell, live life on the edge, is what I say. It was only four little branches after all. I don't really go out looking for trouble but when you're an alien, it takes time to settle in.

Cars can drive you round the bend

Recently, I have come to believe 'Big Brother' is watching. One brush with the law is acceptable, two is downright careless, but three?

Just after the Stavros incident, I attempted to park in the big city. You know what it's like; you spot a gap in a line of cars, only to discover a moped surreptitiously parked in the centre of a prime space. Pauline tells me to drive Greek style, but I just cannot shed years of ingrained, English politeness.

"Stop! There's a space!"

Well there often is, but to go in forwards means parking at an angle, two metres out from the kerb, with your rear end at the mercy of all and sundry.

"Reverse in!"

I tried this once. I stopped, and a bus drew up centimetres from my back bumper. I couldn't reverse.

"He'll pull round," said Pauline giving a weak wristed royal wave out of the window, positive the bus driver would understand and pull out. Wrong. The blast of a two hundred decibel horn made the car shake and me quiver. The bus was going nowhere, except forwards. Umpteen cars queued up behind, and my nerve broke. In a hurry to move off, I stalled the car, only to receive another blast to my eardrums.

I have got a little better. I now grunt and growl and charge aggressively into any potential parking space. In the city, parking is survival of the fittest, which is why I returned to my car to find a policeman writing out a parking ticket. Hell, I was only double parked for ten minutes. I'm always seeing triple and quadruple parking. Why pick on me?

A few days later, while driving along the island's sole highway, I became conscious of a car driving along beside me with a strange man in a blue shirt giving me a wave. I continued driving with CD blaring, when I heard a faint 'bib bib' over Dire Straits. I looked again and the man waving beside me looked a mite peeved. It was then the euro dropped. It was the law - in a sneaky, unmarked car! I sat there while the policeman took his time getting out of his vehicle and leisurely strolling over.

"*Kalimera*," he sneered, from behind dark glasses.

I decided I would probably have a better chance being a tourist, and hoped the policeman couldn't speak English.

"You drive 110. Here only 80."

"Sorry, I'm on holiday. I didn't know," I apologised humbly. The hole I made for myself suddenly got a whole lot deeper.

"Where you rent your car?"

"Er. It's mine."

"Yours? You say you tourist."

He then called his colleague over and there was a lot of deliberation. Would I be lucky? No.

"Passport... father name... mother name."

That was it. Twenty five euros, thank you very much.

CHAPTER TWO

Building our dream

*T*ime was disappearing fast. Storage costs in the UK were piling up, and so was our impatience. And then out of the blue, three months later, Yiannis, the *mechanikos*, paid another visit to the house with a young woman. We all exchanged pleasantries, and then the mystery woman wandered off on her own. She appeared to be extremely inquisitive about our garden.

"Who is she?" I whispered to Yiannis.

"Important lady. Very knowledgeable."

"How long will planning take now?"

"Soon, very soon now. Everything is nearly complete. This lady, she is from the local authority. She has to check your antiquities - if you have them."

The woman had got the bit between her teeth and was now striding purposefully through my peppers and courgettes, seeking clues as to whether the Parthenon was buried under the vegetables. She began poking around behind the chicken house, but finally emerged to declare all was well and she could find no evidence of my having any ancient artefacts. I didn't know whether to be relieved or pleased.

We wished each other *yia sas*, and as they left the *mechanikos* confirmed that the report from the Archaeological Department was the last hurdle to clear and planning permission would be granted very very soon now!

Nothing happened. Soon seemed a very long time. We

waited and waited, and then, early one morning we were rudely woken by a loud crash and a mighty bang!

In my bleary-eyed state I threw open the curtains. Where was blue sky? Everywhere was yellow!

"What is it?" a muzzy voice enquired from under the duvet.

"Don't worry, glyka mou, go back to sleep. There's nothing to worry about."

"What was that bang? Thunder? It's not going to rain - again!"

"No. Everything's yellow."

Pauline woke at once, always concerned about my health - mental or otherwise.

I stood aside to reveal the yellow view. And then, with a roar the earth moved for both of us. And the house!

"*Yia sas*," shouted Giorgos, waving from the cabin of his JCB as it drove past inches from our window.

At last! The start of our new extension!

You don't argue with a JCB. I could see the garden wall had not put up too much resistance. Concrete blocks were strewn over the garden, and it didn't take a huntsman's skill to follow two monster caterpillar tracks crawling alongside the house. With a resounding roar the mammoth bucket sunk its teeth into our functioning, albeit small, cess pit. If there had been a fan in the garden, then everything would have hit it.

"Giorgos! What do we do now?"

His moustache quivered and shoulders shook with laughter. "*Prepei na perimeneis!*"

Wait? At my age you don't often have that choice!

My friend Michalis arrived. He is a master builder - houses, garages, churches, sheep dips, you name it, provided it's in concrete. He was to build our extension. When I pointed out what Giorgos had done, he grinned and clambered up the JCB to direct operations, saying, "Maybe you should not drink or eat much today!"

Clouds of blue smoke swirled around me, as the bucket began its business, which was more than we could do.

Soon there was a five metre hole gouged out of the olive grove, with Michalis busy at the bottom checking that the diameter was a true three metres wide.

A bellow from the lane outside heralded the arrival of a lorry, and on the back of this leviathan sat four huge reinforced concrete rings. These were perilously swung over the house by crane and disappeared into the vast pit behind, stacked, one by one, to be duly covered by a huge frisby of concrete with a large hole in it. The final piece de resistance was a vertical cylinder of concrete.

"What's that for?"

"That is your viewing chamber!"

Viewing chamber? It was hardly riveting entertainment, although my little grandson thinks so. He spends many a happy hour colouring bits of paper, flushing a piece down the loo, then rushing outside trying to spot it being swept down into the bowels of the earth. I suppose it is a novel interpretation on Pooh Sticks.

Surprisingly, everything was dovetailing into place, with Stelios, the plumber, shortly arriving to fit a new sewage pipe, which fed into the vast cavern.

We uncrossed our legs and dashed into the house to road test the new connections.

The following day I found Michalis busily pegging out the extension boundary. This was an exact science based upon years of experience in building crooked houses. Accuracy hinged upon adding up the perimeter measurements on the plan and letting out this measurement on a tape measure. Then, armed with sticks, Michalis surveyed the ground and planted the wood at various points, whereupon he accurately stretched the tape around these guides to create a precise template for Giorgos to excavate.

Was this a cunning mathematical formula devised by Pythagoras? At school I was hopeless at maths, but even I could see this principle was flawed. The building was supposed to be square. However, a diamond shape would also produce the same mathematical result! When I pointed this out to the *mastoras*, I was dismissed with a wave of the hand. He had built houses like this for years. What did I know?

Giorgos began digging, and by the end of the day we had a one hundred metre square - diamondish - two metre pit excavated, with a house surrounded by a huge - I mean vast - pile of soil. We gazed fondly at our open cast mine of a hole. This was the start of things to come.

Moving mountains

I had tried to ignore it, hoping it would go away, but Pauline kept drawing my attention to the hundred cubic metres of soil languishing in the back garden.

"What are you going to do about that?" she kept on saying.

I looked despondently at the two vast, six metre high mountains of soil, desperately trying to be creative.

"We could grow something on it. Make them a garden feature."

These suggestions didn't go down too well.

Perhaps I could spread it around. But swift calculations showed a tsunami of earth would half bury the olive trees, always supposing I could shovel that fast. We'd had a metre high stone wall built all across the back of the olive grove, behind which a sloping terrace ran up to the rock face boundary of our land. I could level the terrace off. All the dirt would fit there a treat.

I looked at the wheelbarrow. It was of traditional Greek design, made of steel and built like a tank - and just as heavy without being filled. I tried a test run, filling it with soil with my English spade, running the barrow over to the wall and shovelling the soil out. I looked over the wall and back to the twin towers. No impression had been made here or there. My heart sank. Where was the cavalry in my hour of need?

Bang on cue, my knight in shining armour appeared - well, tee shirt, shorts and flip flops to be more precise. Thodoris wanted to know whether I could download some Bulgarian music for him off the internet. A deal was done - CD in advance and three crisp 50 euro notes on helping to move a mountain.

The following morning I stood beneath the two mounds, surprised there was no mist swirling around the twin peaks but fully expecting mountain goats to appear over the top. I wore a special leather belt Pauline had bought me. She was worried I might strain myself. It felt as if I was strapped into some strange sado-masochistic device. The buckle was drawn so tight my eyes were popping, but Pauline assured me it had to be like that to give maximum support. Thodoris arrived, also belted up, which made me feel one of the boys. With cigarette clamped firmly between his lips he hammered scaffolding boards together to make a ramp up to the wall.

"Good thinking," I thought. "Time and motion."

Thodoris had a long Greek shovel and sniffed scornfully at my little English one. I bent down, put my back into it and began shovelling, while Thodoris stood ram-rod straight, rhythmically swinging from his hips, as he leisurely swung two shovels to my one. Soon we were both puffing. Me through lack of breath - him on his fag. The barrow was filled. Thodoris spat on both hands and, with a grunt, leaned forward to gain momentum and ran up the ramp with a roar, at the last moment flicking the wheelbarrow over and emptying its contents over the wall.

We repeated the exercise, but this time with me holding the wheelbarrow. I dispensed with the spitting - it didn't seem polite. I grabbed the handles, leant forward, grunted, heaved, strained, and the barrow remained stationery. I set the load down and spat on my hands. It was a procedure obviously designed to oil the wheels of momentum. The load began to move, though at a snail's pace. But I increased speed and we hit the ramp flying, and as I wobbled towards the top, I realised it would be downhill all the way. Summoning every ounce of energy, I reached the top and all the earth, wheelbarrow and I along with

them disappeared behind the wall.

We decided it was probably better if I just filled, rather than wheeled the barrow.

At the end of a sweat-ridden day we didn't seem to have made any inroads at all.

The next morning, Thodoris arrived, bright eyed and bushy tailed.

I felt closer to my work, partly due to being bent double.

"You should use Greek shovel. See? No backache."

Preferring my tried and tested English spade, I prayed work would lubricate my seized up muscles.

We shovelled and barrowed for six days, until, on the seventh, there was light, where before had stood only darkness. Seven kilos lighter, I had discovered the perfect diet!

Bee off with you

Everything was going swimmingly with the new extension, although work appeared to be more of a leisurely breaststroke than a power crawl.

The stakes and strings mapping the foundation lines had long since disappeared, and the black hole now seemed a little eccentric, with no length parallel to its opposite neighbour. Wooden shuttering erected around the vast pit only made matters worse. Designed to receive copious quantities of cement, this vast jelly mould veered off at various angles - none of which came remotely close to ninety degrees.

No matter. Today was the day for knitting.

There was Big Alekos, a bear of a man from Bulgaria, and Thodoris from the same neck of the woods but with more street cred - his baseball cap set at a jaunty angle and sporting a faded, fake Calvin Klein tee shirt. In charge was moustachioed Michalis, who whipped the workers into a frenzy with his fog horn voice. A decibel charged string of abuse is just the ticket for a 7.30 wake up call. Big Alekos jumped down into the pit with all the grace of a dancing hippopotamus. His ample six pack of quivering blubber cascaded over generous cut down denims and wobbled as if it were jelly on a plate. Thodoris nimbly followed suit, and soon all three were knitting lengths of twisted steel into place with ties of wire to create a series of honeycomb metal squares.

Our intrepid trio beavered away, quietly knitting wire until this idyll was broken by sudden cries of pain from Big Alekos. The big man didn't live up to his image and seemed to be a bit of a Jesse. Panic ensued as he hip hopped in a surreal hop scotch across the squares, clutching the back of his neck. Clambering over the wooden shuttering, he stood on the veranda with tears streaming down his face.

I never know where my wife gets this sort of information, but I was despatched into the garden to dig up an onion with instruction to cut it in half.

I returned to find Alekos sitting with eyes tight shut and Pauline armed with tweezers in the throes of a delicate operation. In triumph she held the tweezers aloft, but the satisfaction was short lived as she had her patient's comfort to consider. She proceeded to rub the onion on the wound made in the back of Alekos' neck. Soon his whimpering stopped. The onion had worked its magic. The pain was gone. He was cured! He could work!

Alekos had been stung by a bee - and ten minutes later so had Thodoris. We were getting the flak from swarms of dive bombing bees intent on stinging. Michalis was no fool and didn't want to be the next target. They all downed tools.

Ten minutes later we recognised his dulcet tones echoing around the mountains complaining in no uncertain terms to the 'friendly' neighbour who had placed his hives above our garden. The next day the bees were removed and once again work edged forward, ever so slowly.

With the grid in place, however, doing the washing became a veritable commando course. The laundry room - already tiled and freezer and washing machine in place - was at the far end of the pit, separated from the main house.

Pauline would stagger outside with the linen basket and a step ladder. I couldn't bear to see her weighed down, struggling with a huge, village-style wooden ladder that weighed a ton. So, being a good husband, I bought her a lightweight aluminium version!

She would climb down the ladder into the pit, and then sling the steps over one shoulder, while balancing the bowl of washing and hopping in and out of the Commando course of metal squares until she reached the laundry room and the entrance above her head. Then it was up the ladder, and Indiana Jones all the way through polythene strips of curtain I had hung for protection against the dirt. Unfortunately, the concept failed miserably and the room soon resembled a dust encrusted tomb.

Power to the people!

A week later Kostas arrived to wire the extension and fit a strip light in the kitchen. Interrupted by a delicious smell wafting beneath my nostrils, I paused from my endeavours to write my column. Dinner smelled good, I thought. Caring husband that I am, I called out congratulatory praise on what I took to be forthcoming victuals.

"I'm not cooking anything."

I continued tap-tapping away until a now more pungent odour began rampaging through my nasal passages.

"If you aren't cooking, what am I smelling then?"

Pauline wandered past on her way to the garden, muttering, "You're always thinking about your stomach."

Thirty seconds later I heard a scream. I dashed out to find the meter cupboard with metre high flames shooting out.

"Kostas!!!!"

Showing as much humour as the Grim Reaper, Kostas ambled outside to see what all the fuss was about, while I ran in for something to put out the fire. I helpfully threw Kostas a wet tea towel, which wasn't much help. Water and electricity don't mix so well, do they? No matter, Kostas had an extinguisher in his van. He shot up the garden path with all the pace of a snail sprinting for a lettuce leaf. Minutes later the panic was over, leaving one blackened wall and a huge pool of molten plastic. Without a meter there was no power, but the electricity company surpassed themselves with their emergency service and we were back on within three days.

I thought electric was electric and never knew there were different supplies. Ours was still the original building feed, and thus we have become experienced in the art of conducting - not electricity, but an orchestra of gadgets and gismos. Turn down radiators for the CD to play, and there's always a moment of panic when the dishwasher reaches the 'heat water' cycle. The cordless phone flashes red, signalling there's no power to make or receive any calls. The EPS on the computer begins to bleep as the battery takes over and there is panic while I shut everything down to save losing my work. And throughout this symphony, the lights dim lower and lower, until one of us dashes to the fuse box and cuts the switches in and out to get the right balance of play.

We have come to recognise all is not as it should be when it comes to electricity. Power cuts you can live with. They are inconvenient, but, hey, they make life interesting and reinforce the reason that you shouldn't take everything for granted.

However, it seems mighty strange to me that invariably the power is cut when it's most inconvenient - and always when it's dark. It's as if a game is being played by some divine authority - and it's not the electricity company!

"He's in the toilet. Wait for it... wait for it... now!"

The light goes off, and we spend the next five minutes rummaging around in pitch black, blindly searching for matches and candles, which always seem to have a life of their own, turning up in the most unlikely of places. And then what happens? As soon as the room is aglow with the romantic flicker of candlelight, the power comes back on.

One power cut lasted longer than usual. A lot longer. In

fact, so long we went to bed, woke up and the power was still off. Thirty six hours elapsed, and Pauline idly asked, "You did, of course, re-set both trip switches?"

"Both?" How was I to know there was a trip switch on the fuse box and another on the meter? I'm only a man. We're not supposed to be that clever.

A year ago we had visited the electricity board and applied for a three phase electric supply. We were told it would take six months. There was nothing to pay until the work was completed. Nine months later we were told the work hadn't been done because we hadn't paid. We then paid, only to be told there were more deserving cases, and installation would take a further three months.

Maybe soon we won't need to conduct the electricity, or have to check the trip switch - wherever that is - and life will become less interesting.

Water, water everywhere

The building work continued to poodle along nicely. Walls were rendered, floors were tiled, electrics were connected and plumbing was nearing completion.

I was doing a spot of gardening when suddenly I heard Pauline calling. Having been married for thirty seven years, my subconscious instinctively regulates such calls on a Richter scale ranging from an innocuous, 'tea's ready,' where I can take my time, to a blood curdling, 'there's a spider!' This means, 'get here quick, on pain of death!'

This scream was definitely off the Richter scale.

I arrived into the kitchen with a slip stream of trailing mud. I felt this was a sufficient emergency not to lose valuable time in trying to take off my boots. I found Pauline paddling around on all fours, looking for something. I instinctively felt this was not the time to ask why she was swimming around in the kitchen - Niagara Falls was pouring out from beneath the sink.

"What's the matter?"

This innocuous query, in the circumstances, evoked a somewhat colourful response.

Over a mind-soothing cup of tea, after we had mopped and dried the kitchen and bathroom floors, we discussed what could be done. The mains cold water pipe had burst, it was Good Friday and we were expecting twelve friends on Easter Sunday. As luck would have it, our rescuer presented himself in the shape of young Giorgos, home from college for the holidays.

"No problem, my father has a spiral. I will come back and fit the new pipe."

Minutes later he returned, armed with the new pipe and a mole wrench. He disappeared beneath the sink, only to emerge shaking his head.

"We have to remove the tap."

He wrestled with the chrome fitting, without effect, before adding more muscle by fitting the mole wrench. With a grunt and a wrench, it turned - and the chrome collar broke! No matter which way, the nut holding the split pipe just would not budge. We thanked Giorgos for his efforts, and resigned ourselves waiting until after the holidays for a plumber and, now, also buying a new tap.

Later in the day we took a drive out in Ruby, our old Panda, who was all bright-eyed and bushy-tailed after having had a full service. Returning from a walk, we found all her lights on, and I couldn't switch them off. Spooky! There was still enough juice in the battery to start the engine though. The massive 750cc leapt into life with a roar and a rumble. I glanced down at the dash, and the temperature gauge was showing red. I couldn't turn off the lights, and the indicators wouldn't work. We drove off, and fifteen minutes later after driving over a pot hole all the lights went out and normal service, once again, resumed.

This was not a Good Friday. More expense to shell out at the garage.

Arriving back home, I retired to the garden to take my

frustration out on the jungle of weeds which was threatening to take over. I was brought to an abrupt stop by, yes, a piercing scream that silenced the cicadas.

"Oh no! Not again!"

Back in the kitchen I found Pauline on the floor, on her back, with a hand up the back of the kitchen sink. Naturally the floor was flooded and I couldn't understand the oaths that were gurgling from inside the cupboard, interspersed with cries of pain.

"Has the tap blown?" I asked helpfully.

"No! It's the hot ....agghhh....pipe this time....agghh!"

I repressed any comments about having a shower in the kitchen and made appropriate sympathetic noises of comfort, which obviously fell on stony ground, or rather sank waterlogged without trace. Pauline managed to turn off the stop cock, despite all the pain from a tankful of hot water pouring all over her, and I came to the rescue with another cup of tea.

I began mopping up when I heard a noise. No, it wasn't Pauline this time, but a high pitched chirrup.

"Look!"

At the end of the kitchen stands our incubator, where Pauline hatches her eggs.

"We have four little ducklings!"

We certainly had enough water to make them feel at home.

Moving to Plan B

At last, we reached the point where the house was far enough along that we could press the button, through agents in Athens, for all our things to be shipped from England. Everything seemed to be going without a hitch... until the paperwork arrived.

Did we have a car in the container? Were there guns? Or drugs? Do customs really expect every self respecting drug dealer to answer these questions truthfully?

However, it was not just a matter of form filling. We also

had to go to the local nick, complete the declaration and get the form duly stamped. Faxing the form to Athens was unacceptable; we had to post the original.

Six days later it had still not arrived. Our container was going to be impounded and storage charged until the vital document appeared. It was touch and go, but thankfully it arrived just as the vessel docked.

D-Day was 8.00am. It was 8.15 when two strangers knocked at the door. They introduced themselves as 'un-packers' from Athens.

"But where's the lorry? How can you un-pack without a lorry?"

"Oh, we don't have a lorry! We came over by ferry. The lorry's coming from the port, at the other end of the island."

We clicked our heels for an hour until we suddenly heard much shouting and revving of a large engine in the village above. The container lorry had obviously arrived - all fifteen metres of it. That's nearly fifty feet in old money.

The driver's cab peered round a hairpin, while the back end was stuck against Christos' outside loo. Thankfully there was no sign of anyone being in residence. With his customary zeal, Michalis had taken charge amidst the mêlée of villagers watching this huge basking whale of a vehicle jamming the entire village. Soon there was a tractor waiting, and then a truck, and then a taxi, and still Michalis barked directions to the driver to go forward, go back, right hand down - asta, asta!

The driver began to sweat, Michalis was becoming hoarse, which was a blessing, the villagers were growing agitated and amidst all the shouting and revving of the lorry's engine, the traffic began hooting.

It was obvious; if the driver managed to swing around one bend, he wouldn't be getting his Leviathan any further - forwards or in reverse. There were two more tight bends to traverse. It would be impossible.

Eventually, the driver descended from his cab to remonstrate with Michalis, and after much arm waving and shouting, it was decided to reverse and park.

Plan B was called for.

This arrived in the form of four Bulgarians and Socrates in his truck. Here was the deal. The Bulgarians would off load the container onto the back of Socrates' truck. They would then drive down to the house and unload it. It would probably take about four trips or so. Yeah, right!

The boys from Athens were obviously not ones to get their hands dirty. They liked the plan. And so proceedings began. I suddenly cottoned on as to why there were so many people around. No surreptitious peeking from behind curtains, this was full, in your face, nosiness. They wanted to see what we had brought from England.

"Oooh - big TV!"

"The sofa's a nice colour."

"I don't like that table."

I left them to it and retired to the house. Fifteen minutes later - in a scene from TV's 'The Hill-Billies' – the truck arrived, laden down with furniture and cartons, on top of which perched waving, cheering Bulgarians, one of whom resembled the Incredible Hulk, complete with tattered shirt. Everything was off loaded into the house, with Hulk carrying cartons designed for two. We lost the plot after five truckloads, when the house began to look like a lost property office.

With the final truckload emptied we were left with the Athenian 'un-packers', busily assembling the bed, after which they made their apologies and said they had to go and catch the ferry back to Athens.

That night we lay in our own bed, surrounded by mountains of packing cases, looking out at a perfectly clear night sky, studded with stars. It was so clear because the carpenter had failed to turn up. The windows and doors would be fitted tomorrow and all was well in paradise.

CHAPTER THREE

Everything in the garden's lovely

I had always viewed the agricultural policy of the European Community as one of senseless waste, but came suddenly to appreciate that if your snout is in the trough, then you snuffle with all the rest! Recently the village welcomed a new, cheap water supply for irrigation. Pre-historic JCB's invaded the village and in their wake snaked a great black hose, which conveniently ended beneath a hedge at the end of our garden.

In some haste three workmen arrived - two months later! One to observe, one to dig a hole, and one to connect the stand pipe. Nothing unusual there then. For a moment I thought I was back in the UK. The next day, water meters suddenly began sprouting as people cottoned on to the cheap water. I asked at the *kafenion* how I could apply for a supply.

Simple. Buy the equipment and fit the meter yourself.

Imagine the furore in the UK if you were to surreptitiously tap into Anglia Water's mains supply. It would probably be a hanging offence!

At the local emporium, weird and wonderful gadgets and tools, centuries old, are displayed cheek by jowl with modern technology in plastic and polypropylene. I delved into old boxes, cartons and plastic trays looking for water meters, which seemed to go from small to reservoir size. I needed help, but whom to ask? This was not B&Q, with name tags and uniforms - everyone seemed to be customers. Eventually I decided an old boy taking money was the one. I explained I had a small holding, and he looked at me pityingly. When I showed him the size of hose I had, he shook his head. I barely measured up to a watering can.

He glanced admiringly at the largest coupling on the shelf, and ran his fingers lasciviously over its dial. That's what you call a water meter. My requirements were pathetically small. He clicked his tongue with embarrassment, as if my order was a threat to his machismo. Sniffing disparagingly, he proceeded to reach into one tray after another for various components. A whole hotchpotch of piping, collars and couplings, nuts and extensions was assembled into a mish mash construction that grew to half a metre long.

Handing me this Heath Robinson contraption, he laboriously began to identify each part's code number before keying the information into his computer, which theoretically consolidated stock control and accounting. Unfortunately, technology fails to appreciate that one finger cannot be expected to speedily identify a particular key when there are so many to choose from. It was thus a full five minutes before everything was entered and the printer was allowed to clatter away a receipt showing the total owed - in drachmas. The clock ticked on as a calculator was consulted and the conversion made into euros.

Later, standing in the ditch with my purchases and various tools laid out behind me, I contemplated what to do. There was no stop cock. I pondered some more and came to the conclusion that if everyone else had managed to fit theirs, it couldn't be that difficult.

I held the meter and assorted piping in one hand, ready to jam it on to the open valve as I unscrewed it. It was now or never - do or die - there was no going back. With my left hand I totally unscrewed the seal. With my right I brought the meter into position. Half the island's water supply suddenly gushed out in a torrent. The meter was wrenched from my grasp and flew into the bush. I put my hand across the flow, emulating the little Dutch boy, but to no avail. Soaking wet and my undercarriage pressure cleaned, I fought against the flood and with superhuman effort managed to couple with the main stand pipe and screw in my meter. Still the water gushed, but this time through a much smaller orifice. No matter. Within my Heath Robinson assembly, a stop cock was thoughtfully provided. Pulling the lever up closed everything down.

I had saved the island from drought.

Later that day, at the *kafenion*, I related my sodden experience and complained of the stupidity in not installing a stop cock to the main water pipe. The locals looked at each other and collapsed laughing.

Finally Nikos managed to gasp, "You should have waited until tomorrow. There's no water on Tuesdays!"

The old boys in the *kafenion* look upon me as a child when it comes to country matters. How would I know how to grow things? What would I know about keeping poultry - or animals? I'm British for God sake. Mind you, perhaps they aren't completely wrong. Pauline often says I often act like a three year old!

The droppings of wise advice

Since we came to the village, this kid has had to sharpen his diplomatic skills, as it is well nigh impossible not to cause offence to someone.

Take Themistoklis, for example. If you have seen the TV programme, 'Last of the Summer Wine', then you will understand why we call him Compo. His feet wallow in oversize wellie boots, torn shorts barely cover dimpled knees and a billowing open shirt displays a more than an ample corporation to all and sundry. His mop of wild jet black hair, day by day, gradually turns to grey - until a new day dawns and his barnet magically reverts back to ebony. It must be some kind of black magic.

Themistoklis believes he works harder than anyone else and every day we go through the same ritual. He wipes his brow and extends an arm to let a droplet of perspiration drip off his finger. He will then wince, lean back with the pain of life and the cross he has to bear, saying, "Perhaps I die tomorrow."

This would be unfortunate. I get paid an occasional Robert for turning on his irrigation water each day. A Robert is a rabbit. However, the other day I got a rise. He gave me a bag of feathered Peaches. No, not some strange fruit - two pigeons.

Every day Compo comes into the garden to inspect our vegetables. Naturally, we are always doing things wrong.

Shaking his head at our glut of courgettes, he exclaimed, "Not good. They need *kopria*, and then you have many more. You come - now - and make bags full."

Themistoklis has a small holding approached by a near vertical track that leads up to a ribbon of land on the mountainside; a dangerous indentation beneath vast overhanging cliffs of rock. Here he keeps pigs. About sixty at the last count, where huge pigs and their litters snuffle around in sties made from old palettes. It is here that the *kopria* is harvested.

I emerged from Vox, his forty year old Beetle, which resembles a farmyard on wheels with a haystack on the roof, and animal feed and rubbish filled to the brim inside. Thankfully, I had remembered a shovel, sacks and a pair of Marigold gloves. This was not a job for bare hands!

Compo pulled open a palette to let out some pigs and proudly pointed to the manure inside, telling me to take as much as I liked. Such generosity! I managed four large sackfuls before I realised they each weighed 50 kilos, but with Compo's help we lifted them onto Vox and returned home.

The following day, as we ringed all the vegetables with pig poo, Michalis appeared. He twirled his moustache knowingly, sniffed disparagingly and shook his head.

"*Kopria* from pigs is too strong! The vegetables will die. Sheep *kopria* is best."

Oh no, not again!

Off we drove in Michalis' air conditioned truck. Well, that's a slight misnomer. There are large holes in the floor. Dust and hot air filled the inside, as we climbed ever higher along a dirt track into the mountains where Michalis keeps his sheep. While he went to feed the animals, I did the business and shovelled brown beads of goodness into sacks. Michalis reappeared eager to demonstrate the bargain I was getting. Plunging his hand into the droppings, he pulled out a palmful of 'raisins' and proceeded to crumble them into powder. Extending a gnarled hand, with yellowing nails, he invited me to sniff.

"See! No smell!"

Yeah right!

"What do we do now?" I asked Pauline, after I had staggered home with the bounty.

Which manure did we favour? We didn't wish to offend Compo, or Michalis. A spot of English diplomacy was called for. Under the light of a full moon we dug in the pig and the sheep poo all around the vegetables and then watered it in, so no evidence remained - apart from the smell. Poo might not smell when it's dry, but take it from one who knows; add water and it becomes a heady mix that you wish to stand down wind from, as far away as you can get!

The following day we had separate visits from our benefactors and were told off by both - but unknowingly they were both in agreement.

"I told you to leave the *kopria* on top and gradually water it in! Your vegetables will die now."

You can't rely on gardening advice these days. There was a bumper harvest of everything. Was it the pig or the sheep poo? We'll never know. I just thank God Kyriakos didn't go past on his donkey!

Too many cooks

However, in the Garden of Eden, life is never easy. I can never do right from wrong.

We planted tomatoes, and I came out one morning to

discover Michalis in the garden doing a demented dance in his wellie boots all over our tender plants.

"You must tread on the roots and then re-cover them with soil. It makes them strong!"

Glad he could be of help, I was left looking at a patch of decimated plants. What could I do? I knew nothing. I was English! I began to water them, hoping they would revive, when Perikles arrived.

"What are you doing? You will kill them! Don't you know? Plants need air to breathe. They will drown."

"But I only planted them yesterday."

With a knowing shrug and a pitying shake of his head, he shuffled off, clearly leaving with the opinion that I was beyond redemption.

Two minutes later Christos passed by. "Stop," he shouted. "There's too much water. Didn't you see the moon last night?"

I shook my head, wondering what that had to do with the price of fish.

"The moon was - *pos to lene* - on its bottom half. That always means rain."

"But the moon is that shape every month!"

"Ah, well." And he gave me a look as if to say, "But doesn't everyone know that?"

Despite not knowing what we were doing, the vegetables began to grow with the life force of giant triffids. We'd plant little sprigs of green, and overnight they'd all work out, put muscle on and by the morning would become disturbingly huge green vegetables, angrily bursting out of the ground. Output became a nightmare. We couldn't keep pace with all the garden produce - not to mention all the cats meowing for nourishment, the poultry needing feeding and the ever-growing plants requiring watering, as vast leaves visibly unfurled and crept ever nearer the house. To make matters worse, in the summer we invariably eat out and don't get round to picking all the vegetables.

Nor do we find time to kill the chickens, and Pauline's

investment in an incubating machine - which chucks out fluffy chicks every twenty one days - has meant we have an endless conveyor belt of fresh meat.

Every morning I wake up in a cold sweat from a nightmare; we are disappearing beneath a rising tide of concrete and discarded building materials, and all the time the poultry and animals are clucking and whining for food, while the triffids gradually take over the world.

Stop!!!

The solution was staring us in the face. Self sufficiency!

We got back to normal - almost. The triffids were cut down to size. Bounties of courgettes, peppers and aubergines, which had all grown to marrow size, were now cut - so too were the marrows, which were as large as water melons. The water melons were no problem - they just burst. We cut everything into bite size morsels and fed them to the chickens. We then hit a slight problem with the ducks. They didn't seem to want to join into this new scheme of things. I suggested we feed them oranges - it would save time later, but this didn't go down too well with Pauline, especially as citrus fruit was an extra expense and did not come within our redress of vegetable control.

At the time, chickens had seemed a sensible idea. They are a cheap source of meat, plus eggs - a very village-like thing to do. We were very proud of ourselves, building a little house for the chicks, and when they grew up, a big house with drop-down doors and little perches.

"I suppose you'll be wanting curtains next?"

Was Pauline being patronising?

"No. Chicken wire will suffice," I flounced.

The chicks grew and now, after several months, were fully fledged with cockerels crowing at four o' clock in the morning and chickens clucking and a-laying.

Eggs and tonic

We ran into another over-production problem.

I was frightened to open the fridge for fear of being buried by an egg avalanche. When we were running at five a day, a five egg omelette was manageable - but day by day this became ever more of a struggle. I got egg-bound and God knows how high my cholesterol level reached. Something had to give - and it wasn't me! We couldn't face another egg, no matter how it was cooked, but the chickens kept on laying. Then the bounty increased to ten a day and we lost control entirely. We couldn't give them away for love nor money, as everyone in the village had their own chickens.

My cousin Pam lives in a Portuguese village and is always a font of useless knowledge. I e-mailed her.

She advised me to whisk up each egg and pour it into an ice cube tray. Apparently this freezes perfectly for future use. I dread to think of the reaction of friends, when I mistakenly serve whisked up egg floating on the top of their gin and tonics! However, Pam ignored the core problem. So, OK, we invest in dozens - no hundreds - of ice trays and then what do we find? Yes, we have plenty of room in the fridge - but we have to buy an industrial freezer just to keep up with the frozen egg output!

And then we found the perfect solution.

A chance conversation with the greengrocer in town led him to ask whether we would supply him with eggs - for cash. Before you could say poached, or fried, I scrambled home to return with our current stock of forty five eggs. In exchange, a crisp five euro note was planted in the palm of my hand. Problem solved. With production likely to peak at around 150 a week, we were in the money. Whoever would have thought it? Us becoming egg farmers!

Later that day I was laying a fire in the somba, using some old copies of the *Athens News*, when Pauline came in, with those dreaded words:

".....I've been thinking."

I pretended not to hear. Thirty seven years of marriage has taught me to keep my head down when those words are uttered, for it always means me having to do something I'd

much rather not.

"Chicken eggs are OK, but we need to think bigger."

I scrumpled up the newspaper.

"I read it somewhere. Now what was it?"

I was way ahead. I knew! Desperately I fought to get the newspaper into the somba and light it before it was too late.

"It was in the *Athens News*!"

I slammed the door shut. "What was, light of my life?"

"Ostriches. It had a feature on keeping ostriches!"

I shook my head regretfully and pointed to the fire, shrugging my shoulders apologetically, foolishly believing this would be an end of the matter - but no.

"It'll be on the *Athens News* website."

Don't you just hate all this technology?

So, there I was, surrounded with downloaded information sheets on how to breed ostriches, having been assured we would only start with a ménage-a-trois of two females and a male, but knowing it would be the thin edge of the wedge. The field will be sorted and before I know where I am, I'll be sent off, down to the builder's yard to get the fencing. We logged on to find an egg supplier and found an ostrich farm in the midwest of America. That's the trouble with the world wide net - it's worldwide.

Don't you just love technology?

It seems ostrich eggs are an arm and a leg! I could relax - until the next idea looms.

The chickens are meanwhile pecking away one end while at the other a deep layer of guano is building up, ready to be harvested. It is brilliant fertilizer for the garden and certainly more than a match for sheep, or even pig poo. It all goes to keep the self sufficiency wheels even more well-oiled!

I woke up the other day to a distant cheep, cheep. Bleary eyed, I thought a bird had got into the house, but then remembered it must be from Pauline's magic box, the incubator from where we start our food chain, with fluffy, cuddly chicks, which become meat on feet five months down the line.

However, this batch was a change from the norm - Indian Runners!

Now, probably, this means absolutely nothing to you. I can't even begin to imagine there could be a fellow kindred spirit, who not only has an incubator, but also knows what Indian Runners are. If there is, perhaps we could form a club?

Anyway, it all started a month ago when our wayward son arrived from the UK with a gift for his Mother.

"Here you are Mum - six Indian Runners!"

It was a small box; Stuart was obviously not being particularly generous. Surely it couldn't be awful, limited edition replicas of six, thimble-sized Red Indian tribes?

"Oh, this is just what I wanted!"

Perhaps it was a book about the Indian Raj? Maybe even a cookery book on curries - mmmm.

Pauline began to unwrap the box.

Didn't Agatha Christie write a book with a politically incorrect title. Wasn't it renamed something about six little Indians? Could that be it?

Pauline unwrapped three tea-towels packed inside the box and revealed the precious contents. My expectations were dashed. They were bloody eggs - as if we didn't have enough!

For the uninitiated: apparently Indian Runners are ducks, which stand upright when they run.

But enough of eggs.

One foot in the grave

I was awarded the chore of digging the garden to get it ready for us to plant vegetables and fruit trees. I got as far as looking at the stretch of ground, and groaned. It seemed the size of a football pitch. I pictured the hours of sweated labour involved. It was all too much; a beer was called for. It all seemed extremely daunting - but then I suddenly remembered Alekos. He had a rotavator! A call was made and Alekos promised to call by that evening.

Four days later - which is pretty quick - he finally arrived, just as I was running out of excuses to Pauline as to why I hadn't started digging yet. Alekos proudly patted his ancient machine and pulled on the starter motor. A week of back breaking digging was about to be eaten up in three hours...except the rotavator refused to start.

However, after much cursing, kicking, tweaking and shaking, thankfully it chugged into life. Soon Alekos was happily tilling away, and I was just congratulating myself on having found a less arduous way of digging the garden when I heard much shouting and cursing. I looked out of the window to see Alekos ducking this way and that for fear of being hit by chickens flying everywhere.

Alekos had forgotten vital instructions.

As the rotavator chugged along, so it was wresting buried chickens from their graves, in various states of decomposition, that were sent flying, zombie-like, all over the garden.

He had entered the pet cemetery!

We had been losing chickens to a luritha, a savage, ferret-like animal that seems to kill for enjoyment and then sucks its victim's blood. Is that ghoulish or what? I had buried the remains of ten chickens, dotted around the garden at various intervals, and Alekos appeared to have brought them back to life, catapulting them into the air from the blades of the rotavator.

The massacre had started like this:

Cheep, cheep. Those damned ducks must have hatched.

I crawled out of bed and the cheeping ceased as I approached the incubator. All the eggs seemed intact, but one could have hatched and fallen into the water tank designed to keep the humidity at perfect hatching temperature. I removed all the eggs and peered underneath. Nothing. Was I dreaming? I went back to bed.

Ten minutes later I was just dozing off when I heard cheep, cheep. I turned over. I had had it with birds.

You may be interested to hear that those ducks continued

cheeping intermittently for a few days until I discovered it was the audible warning to renew the smoke alarm battery!

Chickens are always on the move, and when you have over thirty it's very difficult to do a head count, as they keep on moving. Consequently, it took a little time before I began to realise we didn't seem to have quite as many chickens as I thought. Plummeting egg production should have given me a clue.

Then, one morning I discovered the grisly remains of a chicken caught on top of the wire fence. There was literally a skeleton with wings and a pair of claws. The chickens weren't going AWOL. There was something about that had a taste for poultry.

We have thirty chickens and a pen of twelve young incubator-hatched chicks. While Pauline sees them as cute, fluffy little bundles, to me they're meat on feet.

You can, therefore, imagine how upset I was to discover that our twelve young chickens were disappearing one by one. And there, beside an olive tree on the other side of the wire fence, was a large hole. Was the culprit a rat? Or was it that strange, mink-like animal, the luritha?

I was sitting in the *kafenion* when Derek walked in. I explained that food was literally being taken from my mouth. I had now lost five chickens. Derek is never happier than when sharing in some morose tale and empathising with calamities that can befall you in life.

"I know what you can do. A few years ago, opposite to where I worked, they pulled down a gas depot. Every morning, when we came in to work, you could smell gas. We called the gas board, and they arrived with hi-tech gadgets to check for fumes. They couldn't get these gizmos to register anything, but you could still smell the gas! Oh, we don't use our noses for smelling gas, that's unreliable, they said. These monitors were supposed to sense fumes, one unit to umpteen billion parts of air. So they went away convinced there was no gas. Anyway, one morning I had to burn some rubbish and my mate - having a laugh - kicked some burning cardboard over a drain. Well, I saw the draught suck the ember down and ran. I could hear a hissing noise, underground, shooting this way and that. There was a huge rumble. All hell let loose. I was hiding behind the back of a car, when a manhole cover shot straight up in the air like a bloody flying saucer. As the gas caught fire, manhole covers began flying all down the street."

"What has that to do with my missing chickens?"

"We put gas down the hole and set light to it."

"Derek. To get to the hole we have to climb onto a metre high wall, skirt round the compost heap and balance our way along fifteen metres, clinging to the wire around the chicken pen like a pair of geriatric ballet dancers, AND carrying a twenty kilo gas cylinder."

"Let's have a beer."

The next day Derek arrived, ready for action, dressed in black, wearing his SAS woolly hat, and clutching a funnel and hosepipe. He crept around the wall as sure footed as Mr Bean on a tightrope. I, meanwhile, entered the chicken pen clutching a shovel and a container of kerosene. We rendezvoused by the 'hole', separated by the chicken wire fence. I threw over the shovel and Derek cleared weeds from around four more holes. Feeding several litres of kerosene, down the hosepipe, into the hole, he pulled out a tissue and lighter. Our intrepid hero then dropped the lit paper and we both ran.

Nothing.

We rendezvoused again. The paper had gone out. A little braver this time, Derek dropped a lit match and it just burned.

"The kerosene has just soaked away. We need petrol. The fumes will be drawn down into the tunnels."

A new strategy was called for.

I waited while Derek went off with the hose to suck out some petrol from my car. Again he braved the wall as niftily as Rudolf Nuryev, but, wearing wellingtons, with a lot less grace. We - or rather Derek - poured petrol down the hole. I took cover behind the chicken house. Derek hid behind a rock. Rolling tissue into a ball, he fashioned a taper and lit it. Standing up he tossed the 'grenade'. Hole in one! There was a huge explosion, flames shot out from one hole, billows of smoke from another, the tree shook, the ground trembled - and nearly all the chickens died of shock.

The next morning I discovered another example of fowl play. So much for Derek's theory. From what I understood, the luritha finds a way in, makes a kill and afterwards it's the rats that come in for a meal.

Folk wisdom

When we first arrived here, I used to think the old boys sitting in the *kafenion* were steeped in country ways and relied on local folklore to make decisions about their animals, olives and growing things.

"Will it rain tomorrow," I'd ask over a coffee?

Michalis would look up at the sky and purse his lips before turning to Alekos for a second opinion. "Just a few showers?" After much deliberation, Alekos would give a shrug and concur. The others would nod sagely. Invariably they were right. Perhaps they used seaweed. I knew Nikos had arthritis; perhaps his joints could sense impending dampness, or maybe it was something to do with the waxing and waning of the moon. It wasn't until much later that I discovered the ways of the countrymen and was let into the secret. Check the weather forecast on TV!

Thus I have come to understand that one shouldn't totally rely on folklore. You can't be sure whether opinions are being made up - people don't really have a clue - or it's all pure guesswork.

So one morning I sat with the lads at the *kafenion*. Well, lads is a slight misnomer as most are in their seventies, but between them they have a wealth of experience in country ways. After one or two *tsikoudies*, conversation began to flow.

It's small wonder really. To say *tsikoudia* is high octane is a slight understatement! The crystal clear spirit is distilled in the village every October, using the remains of grapes used in the annual wine making.

My mates clucked into their *tsikoudia* - as I recounted the problem in hand.

"You've got a luritha there, Michali," exclaimed Andonis. "That's a big problem."

I knew what the problem was, but how to solve it?

"Put poison down," advised Nikos.

This didn't seem a good idea - not in a pen full of chickens and Pauline's twelve cats wandering around!

"I know," shouted Alekos, enthusiastically. "Line the fence with chicken wire and build a roof. That will stop it getting in."

I pondered this solution. It had merit, but with a pomegranate and two lemon trees growing in the chicken pen, construction could well prove a problem.

Themistoklis then came up with the perfect answer, or so he thought.

"Get a chair, put it in the chicken pen at night, sit on it, wait, and then shoot the bugger!"

Everyone beamed at this perfect solution. I thought for a moment. Firstly, it would be damned uncomfortable and, secondly, if the animal was half as canny as everyone believed, then it would catch my scent and not venture anywhere near. Thirdly, and by far most importantly, it would be pitch dark and I wouldn't be able to see a thing, even with my glasses!

So much for local advice. We'd lost eight chickens. It wasn't funny. This was war.

And then inspiration came from an unexpected source. Sylvia, an English friend from the next village whose sole farming experience, in another life, was shopping at Tesco.

"It could be worth trying a light out there. You never know, it might keep the thing away."

"How do you know?"

"Listen, mate, I was educated at Cambridge. We know one or two things there."

"Did you get a degree in zoology?"

"No, I went to Cambridge Secondary Modern for girls, but it seems common sense that nocturnal animals prefer the dark."

The next night I strung up an economy bulb, which dangled down off the pomegranate tree. It lights up the whole of the pen, and at two in the morning you can see the chickens strutting around as if it's mid-day. But at least they're safe and sound now - the luritha has given up.

God bless Cambridge Secondary, and Sylvia!

Why did the chicken cross the road?

Now that we weren't losing the chickens, it was time for the killing fields.

Oh, don't go all squeamish on me! I don't enjoy the job, but someone has to do it.

Before I lost my virginity I checked out what had to be done in a book on self sufficiency. It went into minute detail on how to wring a chicken's neck. For my first time, I caught a bird and followed the instructions.

"Grab the legs with your left hand, and the neck with your right hand, so that it protrudes through the two middle fingers...."

I grappled with the clucking thing, and got everything into the appropriate position.

"... and the head is cupped in the palm. Push your right hand downwards and turn it so the chicken's head ..."

There I was, with a struggling chicken in one hand, the book in the other and the crucial instruction was on the next page! What could I do?

I gave it up as a bad job and used an axe.

You may be interested to know - to save buying the book - you are advised to bend the chicken's head backwards but stop as soon as you feel the backbone break or you'll pull the head off

Either way, the saying running around like a headless chicken turns out to be more a case of bouncing around like a demented space hopper!

To eradicate this unpleasant part of the execution, I came up with an idea, which was why I was out in the car on a quest. I drove for miles without seeing one. And then, it was just like buses - you wait for hours and suddenly three come along all at once. I rounded the bend and there, in the distance, I saw them - about twelve. I looked in my mirror; there was nobody behind and no houses around. I pulled up, sneaked out, grabbed one and slung it into the car. I was just about to leave the crime scene when I remembered Michalis. He thought it was a good idea, and he wanted one too. Thinking I might as well be hung for a sheep instead of a lamb, I ran across the road and grabbed another one. I burned rubber and made good my getaway.

Safely back home, I carried my bounty into the house.

"What have you brought those in for?"

"It's for the chickens," I declared. "It's a new system."

"But they're traffic cones," said Pauline.

Patiently, I explained that while they may appear to be traffic cones, they were, in fact, a technological advance. Instead of decapitated chickens bouncing around the garden, matters would now be conducted with a little more decorum.

I sawed the end off a cone and went out to catch a chicken. I encountered a few teething problems. If too little was taken off, the chicken's head couldn't poke through: Too much and the bird would fall out. I made one or two adjustments and was soon ready for a dress rehearsal.

I dropped the chicken into the cone. A perfect fit! The chicken was despatched and the cone prevented all the normal flapping about. It was a small step for a chicken but a giant step for mankind.

I went in for a well deserved coffee.

Little Bo-Peep

We were growing succulent vegetables, rearing our own organic chickens and ducks. Was this the good life, or what? Although...we could think a tad bigger, couldn't we?

"Why don't you keep a few sheep? I'll kill them for you," said Michalis.

We went up the mountain to where he kept his flock, and Pauline confidently selected four animals. I was impressed; I didn't know my wife had hidden talents in the finer points of bovine selection. All admiration vanished, however, when I discovered selection had been made purely on colour. I was going to tend four walking rugs, christened Eeny, Meeny, Miny and Mo.

Michalis let me use some land near to our house, and I foolishly presumed it would be a field. It turned out to be the side of a mountain, During my brief induction course as a fully fledged *voskos*, I nervously asked whether I had to milk them. Michalis laughed, shook his head and lifted Mo's tail. The ram baaed loudly at being interfered with around the nether regions, and the other three males nervously backed away.

My next lesson was in buying feed. I basked in the admiration I received at the feedstuff emporium when they discovered I was English and kept sheep, but then I wilted under the three, hernia wrenching, 50 kilo sacks that I had to manhandle into the car.

Next morning, whistling, and with a spring in my step, I strode into the fenced enclosure. I poured feed into a trough, carefully heeding Michalis' warning of not giving them too much or their stomachs would swell and explode. I looked at the meagre rations. I had to get it right. Too much and they'd go to meet their maker - too little and they'd kick the bucket through malnutrition. This kind of stress can give you high blood pressure.

In the corner of the field and lined with rocks, there was an old well. Using a plastic paint tub, I attempted to draw some water. It wasn't easy. You had to drop the 'bucket' at just the

right angle, before it began to fill. There was another handicap
- a hole in the bucket - which meant I lost half the water in the
process of pulling it up, and most of the rest running, well
staggering, from the well to the rusty oil drum, cut in half, which
served as a drink tank.

Gradually, I honed my shepherding skills and even ventured
to supplement the animals' diet with greenstuffs, but it has to
be yellowed and crispy, not fresh.

Checking on my prowess, Michalis met me one morning as
I was staggering under the weight of one week's feed on my
back. I gratefully allowed him to take the sack, which he slung
over his shoulder as if it weighed nothing. Pushing open the
gate, the animals ran towards us and I suffered the indignity
of being savaged by a sheep, as Miny jabbed me with a horn. I
turned back a moment later in horror, too late to prevent
Michalis from emptying the entire contents of the sack into the
feeding trough, defying all the instructions he'd given me about
sheep blowing up. When I shouted at him, he merely shrugged
and instructed me to check the following day, and if an animal
appeared bloated, he'd kill it for me.

Thankfully, all was well, but three days later Eeny and Mo
went AWOL! My mentor said they could have fallen and be lying
injured. I struggled up the mountain, Rambo-like, clambered
over boulders, jumped ravines and tore through brambles, but
in the end had to admit I was really a bit of a Bo-Peep. I couldn't
find them.

However, the next morning after a night out on the tiles,
there they stood outside the fence, happy as Larry. As soon as
I approached, they retreated. I opened the gate to shoo them
in. They stood motionless, giving amused bleats while Meeny
trotted out to freedom behind me. I was supposed to be a
shepherd wasn't I? Self consciously I called *ela, ela*, but to no
effect. I threw a stone just like a real shepherd and hit Eeny on
the head. This galvanised them into action. Realising they were
not up against an amateur, like lambs they all came running
home wagging their tails behind them. Little Bo-Peep, eat your
heart out.

But then came the day.

Michalis arrived with a cleaned out plastic paint tub containing all manner of bits and pieces. We were about to become blood brothers. Pauline had idly said to my friend that the freezer was low, and I was becoming tired of eating poultry. Well, I was about to get a change of diet.

I nervously stood in the field beside Michalis.

"Which one?"

"Meeny," I gulped.

Michalis gave me a sideways glance. "Meeny? *Pios einai* Meeny?"

Who gives sheep names? I pointed a trembling finger at Meeny, who began giving me sheep's eyes, innocently believing I was here to dole out the food. Michalis placed a noose over the animal's head and dragged it away. Sadly I fed Eeny, Miny and Mo before going back home.

Thankfully, Michalis had already done the wicked deed and was busily delving in the tub looking for a pair of bellows. Making a slit in poor Meeny's leg, he pushed a rubber hose beneath the skin and began to pump at the bellows. Gradually Meeny began to inflate until he was huge, with four little legs poking out from a huge balloon. Just before he was due to pop, Michalis stopped pumping and strung Meeny up on an olive branch.

I was impressed. The air had separated the flesh from the skin and fleece. Within a couple of minutes there was our first rug.

"Paulina, she make *loukanika*?"

I like sausages and nodded. For the next five minutes Michalis pulled out yards and yards of intestines, squeezing and pulling and squeezing and pulling, until there was a huge pile of sausage skin on the ground. It was obviously a case of waste not, want not.

Dinner with Anna

So now we had lamb in the freezer. Where was the pork?

I clambered the last few steps up to a strip of land overlooking the gorge. Above, at an impossible angle, towered huge boulders, hanging over the mishmash of assorted pallets arranged as cages.

"*Yia sou,*" waved Themistoklis, a vision of sartorial elegance in lumberjack shirt, threadbare track suit bottoms and wellie boots.

I had foolishly mentioned I'd like some pork for the freezer. To me, pork was always displayed in cling-filmed polystyrene trays, but the meat here was breathing!

Themis let his animals out to eat and chortled, "Anna, you go home with Mike tonight!"

She was a plump little thing, weighing 60 kilos. Anna was a nice name, unlike the impersonal, anonymous "Two Loin Chops" you find at Tescos.

Themis crouched amongst the snuffling, black, hairy bodies to tie a rope around the leg of a squealing Anna. Below me, I saw the Grim Reaper approaching, clutching a wicked looking knife.

"*Yia sou*, Niko!"

Nikos was the local butcher and obviously here to play an important part in the procedure. Without further ado, Themis picked up his gun and aimed. I tensed and closed one eye, anticipating the bang. And then the bloody pig ran towards me. A tirade of Greek curses, English prayers and squealing pig wrought the air. In the cacophony I didn't know whether Themis was barking instructions at me or swearing at the pig. He stood twenty feet away, gun raised. The barrel wavered. I jumped aside. BANG! I turned. Anna had slumped to the ground, and immediately Nikos was upon her with his knife. Did I say her? I had only come for pork but then I met a pig, and now it was a she and she had a name. We almost had a relationship!

Meanwhile, Themis was tying the leg of a large boar to a concrete post. It squealed in fury when Themis reached for his gun, and pandemonium ensued as Nikos and I ran hither and thither to escape being caught in the crossfire.

BANG!

The boar fell, thrashing wildly. The Grim Reaper moved on to him in an instant. He made a slit in the boar's nether region, deftly removing its testicles so fast it made my eyes water. Apparently, removing the testes makes the meat taste sweeter. You don't learn of such things wandering down the meat aisle in Sainsburys

The three of us strained to lift the animal onto a pallet, where it lay still quivering, ready to be skinned and butchered. The sun had fallen below the mountain and dusk was quickly giving way to darkness, as Nikos finished butchering the boar and gutting my Anna.

With a cheerful wave he left Themis and I to manhandle four portions of boar, weighing some twenty five kilos each, onto the roof rack of Vox. My nearly friend was placed reverently beneath the front bonnet.

The old car groaned under the weight. We set off with one of Anna's legs poking from the bonnet, pointing the way and blood dripping down the windows from a hundred kilos of pig on the roof. The whole scene, with a bag of intestines on the back seat and the boar's head wedged between my legs, resembled Nightmare on Elm Street. It began to rain and the wipers smeared red rivulets of blood to and fro, as the chainsaw massacre slowly drove down the mountain with all the speed of a careering hearse.

It was pitch dark when we arrived at our house and it seemed as if Anna had put on some weight as we struggled up the path. Pauline opened the door and was horrified to receive one large roasting joint, complete with feet and head, instead of the more manageable cuts she had been expecting. Themis insisted on bringing Anna inside, but Pauline refused. After a lively debate, a clothes line was duly commandeered and deftly tied around Anna's back leg. Threading the slack over the main strut of our pergola by the front door, we managed to raise Anna, leaving her dangling four feet above the ground. Themis bid us goodnight and disappeared into the darkness, promising to return tomorrow.

We looked at each other, and then at Anna gently swaying in mid-air and thought, oh yeah, and pigs might fly!

The next day there was a pounding on the door. It was seven in the morning and pouring with rain. A drowned Themis stood there demanding, "Where your razor?"

I peered out. Anna was still there, but overnight she'd been to the hairdresser. Yesterday she'd been a sultry dark brown. This morning she was an attractive strawberry blonde! Was this an effect of rigor mortis, I wondered?

We cut the pig down and manfully struggled to carry her over to a large flat rock in the garden, with Themistoklis ranting all the while about Gadaffi and the sand he'd sent from Libya to poison the rain. I hoped this was not some secret weapon and probably just a natural phenomenon.

"The pig need shave now!"

Not with my razor she didn't! With a lot of huffing and grunting it was agreed the alternative was a blow torch. Themis struggled to light it in the driving rain, using a whole vocabulary of words I didn't know but understood perfectly well. With the flame finally roaring, he began to scorch the skin, instructing me to follow on behind, scraping away with a knife to remove the bristles from the pig's little private places. After an hour it was as smooth as a baby's bottom.

Themis fumbled for a heavy cleaver from a bundle of plastic bags he'd brought. I drew the short straw. I had the knife. I had to cut off all the pig's nipples. I think we should draw a veil over what happened next. Suffice to say all roasting joints were filed in INKA bags, chops in Champions' and miscellaneous in a variety of bags from the local baker and building suppliers.

With sixty kilos of pork in the freezer, my pig days were over. I sighed thankfully.

Home surgery!

However, a week later Themistoklis came pounding on my door again. Opening his track suit top, he revealed a squealing piglet, just two days old with a large gash on its leg. We had a

bottle of Tea-tree oil, a natural antiseptic, and Pauline used this
to bathe the wound. Themis was very impressed and marked
my wife down as a budding veterinarian.

The following day he returned with yet another piglet.

"You have needle? You sew!"

Surgery was a little advanced for my current level of
veterinary skills. There was a gaping wound on the piglet's back.
I opted for holding the wriggling, squealing animal and thought
that was being brave enough. Themis pushed the needle through
the skin and began darning. I've never been this close to an
operation before - apart from on television - and then only from
behind a cushion. Sewing the huge flap of skin to cover the
wound proved impossible.

I then had a flash of inspiration. Super Glue!

Themis was extremely dubious. I dropped a bead of glue on
the sides of the wound. The pig squealed, Themis prodded it
and my finger got caught in the middle. In seconds we were
stuck together. He shouted, I swore and the pig cried. Like a
demented crab, we all side stepped our way over to the tap,
where I managed to release us. Themistoklis had no truck with
this newfangled technology. Pigs grafted onto humans were not
his cup of tea and I warned him to keep his hands to himself. I
completed the surgery and the glue held the wound together
perfectly.

The next day he returned. I looked out rather nervously. Not
a piglet in sight! He'd just brought us a gift for helping him - a
bag of eggs! I just hope I don't get a reputation in the village as
some kind of miracle worker. The thought of opening my door
every day to a queue of bleeding animals makes me feel quite
queasy.

However, a few weeks later, an agitated Themistoklis
knocked at the door.

"*Ela!*"

Without any of the normal exchange of pleasantries - "are
you well - yes - and you - ah, not so bad" - he turned and hoofed
it down the path, wellies squelching at every stride, waving us
to follow him. Outside stood Vox, and there in the front

passenger seat sat, what looked like a white haired old lady haughtily gazing out of the window.

"It's her - *pos to lene* - uterus. It's come out!"

I don't do hospitals and the thought of the diagnosis left me feeling a mite queasy. Themis delved in the boot and brought out a concoction he had prepared earlier - a bottle of olive oil and washing up liquid. He was about to do an internal on the roadside! I was only slightly relieved when he opened the car door for the patient to get out, and I discovered the old dear sitting there was actually a pregnant sheep.

Thankfully, I can trust Pauline to take command in these situations. With all her Girl Guide First Aid Badge coming to the fore, she examined the animal, which bleated forlornly at the indignity of it all. Themis prepared himself for the delicate operation, smearing his hands with homespun lubricant, ready to push, shove or ram the misplaced organ back from whence it came. However, he was not quick enough for Pauline. She gripped the unfortunate animal's head between her legs, bent over, grabbed its rear end and stood up, leaving the sheep doing a hand stand. With a loud slurp, the uterus disappeared. Themis shook his head.

"That's no good. It won't stay there. Michali, do you have scissors?"

I brought him a pair from the kitchen.

"Paulina, you are a woman. You know better about these things."

I didn't understand the sudden sense of decorum, but Pauline did as she was told and began trimming the sheep around its nether region. Themis, meanwhile, was delving around in the car looking for something important. With the sheep's backside now exposed, Themis ripped off a length of sellotape, believing a good strapping of tape would do the trick.

Pauline had other ideas and went off in search of curtain lining. Deftly wrapped in lengths of material, the sheep ended up looking like a bizarre Sumo wrestler.

"That's no good," exclaimed Themis. "She won't be able to go pi-pi."

Pauline made suitable and appropriate adjustments, which Themistoklis accepted.

"I very busy. You inject her morning and night. She has two babies. When born, maybe in three days, I give you baby sheep. That's if she does not die."

Themis is not noted for his generosity, and this was a contractual loophole to cover himself having to part up with anything. Leaving us with a huge syringe and a bottle, he waved us goodbye and sped off, leaving us to tether the sheep in the olive grove.

That evening, clutching a torch, we made our way to the olive grove. Pauline filled the syringe and the sheep eyed us nervously.

"Hold its head, and I'll inject her at the back."

The animal did not like this arrangement, as it began to struggle and Pauline nearly injected her finger. This was not easy.

"Hold it tighter, so it doesn't move."

As if wrestling a steer to the ground, I clung on grimly, with arms and legs vainly attempting to prevent the animal from struggling. Thankfully, Pauline separated the fleece, grabbed some skin and injected what appeared to be five gallons of medication.

This exercise continued for two days until the needle bent. I tried to straighten it, but the metal snapped. We told Themis, who was not pleased and complained we must have done it all wrong. Ungrateful *******!!!

The next morning Dolly was gone. Yes, I know it's a girly thing, but we had to call her something.

We didn't see Themis for a week, until he arrived with a plastic bag.

"The sheep died, but I thought you could have these, instead."

Six eggs, as if we had a shortage! His generosity knows no bounds!

Eggs? Did I mention eggs? Pauline was beginning to get the bit between her teeth. If she couldn't have ostriches, how about turkeys?

CHAPTER FOUR

Searching for a lady who wears big knickers

*I*t seemed a good idea at the time. So good, in fact, I could almost smell it! I laid a foundation, ordered plywood and screws, painted the finished result in an eco-friendly green, and surrounded the whole caboodle with a wire fence. Everything was ready. What turkey ever had a more desirable residence?

Excitedly, we went off to the next village to meet a man, who knew a man.

We found him standing in front of a breeze-block building containing a hundred whistling turkeys, all of six weeks old. I know, you thought turkeys gobbled but at this age, believe me, they whistle. We wanted two females and a male, and the breeder pointed out the male had a much wider head. I nodded wisely at this expert demonstration of turkey sexing, but really I couldn't tell the difference between any of them. I just hoped the turkeys could.

We drove home with our brood whistling away as if they were going to a party. As they tentatively explored their new abode I could see one was larger and decided he had to be the male. He was aptly christened Christmas Dinner. The two others we decided to call Plumpy and Eternal. Even at this age they were big birds with a good two foot wing span, although under the feathers they were only sandwich size.

However, our brood had to go through an induction ceremony!

With bodies crouched and arms spread wide we ran round

the compound like headless chickens. The turkeys thought this was great fun and ran and ran. Finally, we caught Christmas Dinner. I held him upside down while Pauline, who is a lot braver than me, cut his wing feathers on one side. If he attempted to fly now, it would only be in low circles. It took half an hour to administer the same treatment to the other two.

It was time for a thirst quencher, and we went inside for a cool beer until we heard an almighty commotion and saw a whistling, flapping turkey careering down the side of the house with a cat in hot pursuit, followed by our barking dog. Before you could say chestnut stuffing, our Christmas Dinner was out in the lane and hopping and skipping down the mountain. We joined the chase. The dog lost interest and we lost all sight and sound of cat and whistling turkey.

Suddenly, two middle-aged cyclists came wobbling round the bend towards us clad in gaudy lycra and pointy helmets. I bid them good morning and politely enquired whether they had seen our turkey. They were on holiday in the middle of nowhere and they treated this inane query as if it were the most normal thing in the world to be asked. They could only be English! Diligently, they thought for a moment, debated with each other and being ever so helpful, declared that yes, they had heard a noise but then thought perhaps it was a sheep. Big help! As two bottoms thrust into the air, powering their machines away, they offered to keep a lookout along the way.

"It answers to the name of Christmas Dinner," I shouted helpfully.

Back at the turkey coop all was not well. Encouraged by Christmas Dinner's flight, Plumpy and Eternal were perched on top of the wire fence, wobbling this way and that, flapping their wings making ready for takeoff. I watched in horror. I could see my investment in festive meals going out the window. I flapped my arms and shouted. They whistled disdainfully at my poor turkey impression, but it did the trick

- almost. Plumpy crash landed back into the pen with all the grace of a frozen, oven ready turkey. Eternal did the opposite and landed outside. I made a grab, caught a leg and dropped her back over the fence. In moments both began pecking away into a fine meal, which looked suspiciously like Paxo.

They are both fattening up nicely and seem to have quelled their quest for freedom. It also turns out that Plumpy is a he and we have re-christened him Bluey. He has grown into a huge male turkey, all of twenty five kilos, with a scrotum head and red wobbly bits. He proudly stands at the entrance to the pens at feeding time, as threatening as a club bouncer, gobble gobbling away, vibrating his flared tail. Inside, the chicks strut their stuff, scratching and pecking, stuffed with a never ending supply of greens. In dark corners with much clucking, rustling and flouncing of feathers, hens are being egged on to get laid.

As for Christmas Dinner, he has never been seen or heard from again and one can only hope the end was painless and that he's gone to that great oven in the sky.

The big knickers

Out in the duck pen I've built a pond. Its shimmering surface of green slime and a dense blackness beneath is much loved by the ducks. In fact, it plays a vital part in their mating rituals and many a duck waddles out of the depths with a shimmy and a shake, a fluffing of feathers and a coy look at the drake as if to say, "thank you so much!"

Early one morning I went into the duck compound to begin my chores. Two ducks feeling frisky before feeding flew into the pond, throwing up a green spray of foul smelling water. Not wish to be a Peeping Tom, I crept discretely around in search of eggs. Ducks lay in a variety of odd places, and it is always a case of hunt the thimble. I collected four - two in each hand. Deciding to take a short cut, I went by the pond and slipped on its slimy edge. My feet shot backwards. Egg-gripping hands flailed wildly in the air. My life flashed before me. Down I crashed, ending up with my bottom half laying in the mucky water and top half slumped on a bed of guano. My arms stood to attention with each hand holding aloft two perfectly preserved eggs.

I slithered out of the murky depths for fear a drake might consider me fair game and squelched to the house. Stripping off my sodden jeans, hip probably broken, blood pouring from my knees, I limped inside looking for tea and sympathy. Pauline merely looked up from reading her book.

"Why go out to feed the chickens in your underpants?"

Was I becoming an underwear pervert?

It has been noticed in the village of late that I have developed a passion for ogling ladies' bottoms.

One morning I took one furtive glance too many, and spotted a grinning Michalis wagging his finger. He assured me it was natural, indeed normal, to look at the derrieres of ladies, providing they were old enough and younger than fifty - alright, if pushed, fifty five. But the widow Katerina, for God's sake, was ninety two!

I reassured my friend that it had nothing to do with age. I checked that nobody else was around to hear and whispered confidentially, "It's size that matters."

Michalis' eyes widened, but they nearly popped when he saw what was in the bag I was holding - the biggest pair of drawers you ever saw. Michalis crossed himself. It was too much for him to bear. I hastily had to explain.

Recently our grand-daughter had come to visit and had fallen madly in love with a village puppy. After much pleading we agreed that the dog could go to England after the statutory injections, tests and six months wait spent with us. The puppy was a delightful bundle of energy with a fetish for stealing things - hence being christened Klefti, "thief".

One morning he arrived at the door with these prize pair of bloomers. Who on earth did they belong to? And so began my quest to solve the mystery. I quickly worked my way through all the ladies of the village - metaphorically speaking, of course - but nothing fitted the bill, or the drawers.

In the end, I had to put the stolen spoils down to a passing tourist. Although what they would have been doing when Klefti ran off with them doesn't bear thinking about.

Our garden became a depository for all manner of weird and wonderful things. Individual shoes, but never a pair, tea towels, carpentry tools, an apron, but never anything so exotic as those mammoth smalls.

Over the months Klefti has grown into a friendly little chap and always accompanies me to feed Eeny and Mo, our sheep. Although, of late, Meeny and Miny have not been eating much - just chilling out in the freezer! Nevertheless Klefti always greets the sheep with a kiss good morning and then lies on his back in the feeding trough, while they lick him before they all tuck into breakfast, Klefti included.

The seven cats that patrol our garden, keeping it a rat and mice free zone, also let Klefti share their food, as do the chickens and turkeys. He isn't exactly what you would call a fussy eater, enjoying a catholic diet of sheep feed, cat food and chicken seed!

Having been 'chipped' for his doggy passport and had a rabies injection, Klefti was now due for a blood test. The vet took a sample and we waited patiently while the centrifugal machine separated the blood for analysis. Five minutes later a worried looking vet emerged holding a phial. It was evident something was seriously wrong.

"See? These are red corpuscles, these are white ones and this should be clear plasma but it's solid white. I've never seen anything like this in my life."

Was Klefti ill? But he was as bright as a button and so full of life. Could there be a mistake? The vet took another sample. He shook his head. "It's almost as if its solid fat."

I looked at Pauline and simultaneously we both exclaimed, "the pig!"

After cutting up a side of pork in the olive grove - as one is wont to do - I had thrown all the trimmed fat onto the compost, only to discover half an hour later that Klefti had gorged himself on a kilo or more of pig fat!

We took Klefti home fully expecting him to be as sick as a dog. He obviously had the digestion of an ox, though, for the next day after another blood test he was declared A1 fit to travel and start his new life in colder climes.

A wild wool rave

Village life can invariably lead to unusual, nigh strange, social occasions.

We'd been invited to a party. We drove to the venue way up above the village where it was wild and barren. Arriving at a series of dilapidated breeze-block buildings, I thought, "could this be a rave?" Outside, I was greeted by a bouncer, Michalis, dressed in cowboy chaps.

I followed him into the dark bowels of a building, which housed many of the other revellers who had already arrived. Debauched on bottles of *gazoza*, we drank and toasted ourselves. Once our numbers had swelled to twenty or so, Michalis judged it was time to party. We felt a little under-dressed in shorts and sandals compared to the others, who all seemed to be wearing two pairs of trousers. We followed the leader through a door into a dark, dank room, which could have been a speakeasy for all I knew. Suddenly a metal door opened and a blinding light cut through the blackness, followed immediately by hordes of bleating sheep. What sort of perverted party was this?

I could see the room was divided by a row of feeder troughs. The sheep were crammed into one half of the room, while all the partygoers stood in the other. This was no party. This was work!

A team of pickers manhandled sheep to the floor and tied their legs together. Bundles of sheep were then passed along the row until we all had an animal each. I was handed a wicked pair of scissors. I looked down at my sheep. It returned my stare with a forlorn expression. Did it have a sixth sense and knew the only thing I had ever trimmed in my life before, was my nose? We were both frightened, although I could see the sheep had suddenly become far more scared than me.

The darkness was filled with bleating, clipping, cursing and shouting, as a warm, fetid smell hung heavy on the air. This was not Australia, where electric razors neatly skim a fleece off and down to the skin in fifteen seconds. This was more of your rough hedge clipping with rusty shears, leaving the sheep with a whole range of nightmare haircuts, from short back and sides, to the more off the wall, Mohican look. The expert beside me was on his tenth animal as I tentatively rolled my sheep over to do the other side and gingerly began to snip away round its nether regions. By the time I had finished my one, everyone else had sheared around eighty sheep, which were now running around footloose and fancy free.

Now it was time to party! Out came tables and chairs and in came the wives holding big bowls of food. Cold beers were pulled up from the well, the nearest thing to a fridge this far from the village. Bread was cut, salads prepared and we all sat down to be served huge dishes of lamb and pilaffe.

Great chunks of meat and bone sat cheek by jowl for all to pick and choose from. The head was reserved for Michalis. Nudging the man beside him, mine host pulled out his knife and neatly cut out an eye from the skull. Everyone thought it was very funny and laughed uncontrollably when he proffered this tasty morsel to me. I couldn't see the funny side myself. It was only an eye for God's sake. I took the knife, opened my English, stiff upper lip and clenched the eyeball between my teeth. Pausing for greater effect, a hush fell over the room, broken by huge cheers when I rolled it around, chewed and swallowed - and very tasty it was too!

The beer flowed, as did more and more plates of lamb and pilaffe, all rounded off by huge wedges of watermelon. Stuffed to the gunwales, I could take no more. And then, when I thought it was all over, out came miscellaneous water and soft drink plastic bottles, all containing *tsikoudia*.

"*Tou chronou!*"

Next year! It was all I could do to think about tomorrow's hangover, let alone drink to the next sheep shearing party!

A proper English Christmas dinner

Later in the year I got my own back.

It seemed like a good idea, introducing our village friends to a traditional English Christmas. Unfortunately, many key ingredients are not available on the island. Therefore, we had to be a little creative!

Pauline set to, making a cake mix that wallowed tipsily in Metaxa for a month. And then the problems began. Marzipan? Mincemeat? Sausage meat? Stuffing? Not 'ere mate!

The marzipan problem was relatively simple - fresh almonds, finely crushed in the blender and mixed with sugar and, proudly, our own chicken eggs.

Mincemeat was impossible without the key ingredient - beef suet - but Pauline had the Christmas bit between her teeth, and no amount of explaining to the local butcher could make him comprehend that this mad woman needed minced beef fat to go in a spicy jam, which is put into little pies! Wearily, he did as he was told and Pauline was so grateful she threatened to bring him some mince pies. We left him behind the till, desperately praying he would not be offered one of these terrible English concoctions.

Two days later, he thought his worst nightmare had arrived when Pauline returned! She seemed quite normal, asking for two kilos of pork mince. However, not that normal, as it had to be put through his mincer three times. Mixed with toasted breadcrumbs, lemon zest and herbs picked off the mountain, we had the perfect sausage meat for stuffing the turkey and making sausage rolls.

The turkey was my job. Christmas Dinner had done a runner, and the remaining babies had snuffed it, but we still had two birds - Bluey and Eternal, which was an unfortunate name in the scheme of things. I didn't fancy tackling Bluey with his blue scrotum of a face and red dangly bit jauntily covering one eye. The end was nigh, then, for poor Eternal. She weighed a massive twelve kilos! I did the business and triumphantly brought the bird into the kitchen, duly trimmed of extremities and devoid of recognisable features likely to make Pauline emotional.

With a Hanibal Lector stuffing of Eternal's liver, chopped with herbs and breadcrumbs, she was duly stuffed and reverently placed into the oven on Christmas Eve to cook very slowly throughout the night. She just fitted in the oven with the pan perched precariously on the runners.

Early Christmas Day, clad only in a pair of socks - I find tiles a little on the cold side for my feet - I got up to check the bird. As I struggled with the pan, fat spilled out. There was a huge roar. Not sure whether to save the turkey or my credentials, I felt like Indiana Jones as an enormous fireball spewed out of the oven. It was all over in seconds, but Eternal and I both came out of it unscathed - well, she was cooked to a tee, and I just nearly cooked.

Everything was perfect for a real traditional Christmas when we sat down with our friends. They had brought a casserole of pork with them, in case everything went pear-shaped and they didn't take to English food. They'd tried turkey once before. It had been boiled for pilaffe, chunked and served tough and cold. However, this was different. Eternal was going down a treat.

I picked up one of the crackers we had brought from England and held it out to Michalis, who didn't know what to do. We explained it was an English tradition. Pull it and it goes bang - and there's a gift inside.

"Oh, look - a plastic moustache!"

Michalis looked blank and tweaked at his real one.

See. There's a paper hat inside. We all have to wear one! (I passed on translating cracker jokes into Greek!)

We all sat there in our silly paper hats and I wondered why

on earth do we all do that? Perhaps we're mad? Eccentricity, however, is not just for the English!

On Christmas Eve we had gone to a church service with a thousand other people crammed into a vast cave. There was a beautiful Nativity scene with real animals tethered around the crib. A calf, a baby goat, lambs and, oh yes - an ostrich! Enough said!

CHAPTER FIVE

Greeks bearing gifts

I sometimes wonder whether we are a source of entertainment to the village, always being presented with strange gifts at strange times as if we are participants in some strange game show. However, I have come to learn that you never look a gift horse in the mouth.

Eggs are a favourite gift, invariably pressed upon us on the way to the airport. Have you ever tried carrying twenty eggs in your hand luggage? We are obviously seen as creatures with high cholesterol tolerance, for a gift of eggs, while somewhat gratefully received, are coals to Newcastle. Everyone knows we have chickens of our own, and eggs coming out of our ears.

Wine is a very welcome gift but, as usual, nothing comes easy. Nikos presented us with two, twenty five litre containers of his wine but explained he wanted the containers back that week. I like a drink, but this was a drop more than I could cope with.

A wooden barrel was the answer but, unfortunately, this has to be cured before use. For the next three days this meant going down to the cove, clambering over rocks and emptying and filling the barrel with seawater, after which I had to bring the cask back up to the house to refill it with fresh water. Finally, after a further twenty four hours this was emptied and a cheap bottle of brandy poured in. Then, and only then, could the barrel be used and the containers returned, leaving me in need of a well earned drink.

An excited Giorgos called out to me one day: "Michali, do you want salt?" I must have looked mildly interested because he added, "Hurry, I've seen some."

What was all the fuss? Was there going to be a shortage at INKA? Was it on offer? Did I need my Loyalty Card? When he told me to bring a spoon and bags, I wondered if we were going to break in. But no, we drove to the sea and behind a mountain of rocks I was shown a pool encrusted with natural sea salt. This was where the spoon came in handy, and we gathered enough to last the year.

Presents can be a little more surreal. I was called to the gate one afternoon to where Andonis was standing, stripped to the waist, holding a bucket. It was full of freshly caught sea urchins. Instructed to hold out my hands, he placed six of the moving creatures onto my palms, telling me to cut the bottoms off with a knife and to spoon out the inside. He left chuckling, which no doubt meant - let's see what you make of that.

However, the piece de resistance must go to Themis, who turned up with a newly born lamb.

"Here. Present. No money. It will probably die."

The negotiation

In the village you never look a gift horse in the mouth, but you don't always get something for nothing.

It seemed a good idea at the time - buying land next door. We knew it wouldn't be a gift, but we hoped it would be a steal, which is why we let Roxannie into the secret. We may be cabbage looking, but we're not that green.

"Don't tell anyone, but it would be nice to buy the olive grove next door for our children."

When it comes to gossip, Roxannie is world champion. A secret told in confidence is broadcast around the village faster than the speed of sound.

Two days later a nonchalant Manolis knocked on the door. "*Yia sou*, Michali. I was just passing when I had a wonderful idea! I thought my olive grove would make the perfect place for your children to build a house. Come. I show you. It is only next door."

I followed Manolis, and we tramped around trees and through undergrowth with Manolis all the while pointing out every salient topographic feature. It seemed irrelevant that we had lived next door to this land for years and knew it as well as he did. At the end of the ramble Manolis was looking for a reaction.

"Good land, yes? Listen, you are my friend so I will give you very good price?"

"Oh, I don't know. How much is a good price?"

"Sixty."

"Sixty what?"

"Sixty every square metre."

I bid him good evening, hinting that I might be interested, but we didn't have that much money.

Two weeks went by and as we drove out of the village I met Manolis coming the other way in his truck. He drew alongside.

"*Yia sou*, Michali. I have been thinking. About the land. You remember?"

I nodded, noticing I now had two cars behind me and another fast approaching Manolis.

"Sorry, sixty was too expensive."

"Do not worry, Michali. I help you. Thirty is very good price," and he offered his hand through the window to clinch the deal. In the meantime, the other drivers had become impatient and a cacophony of hooting urged us forward. I shook my head, waved and drove on.

A week later there was a knock at the door.

"*Yia sou*, Michali. I have been thinking. Maybe thirty is too much for my land."

"Yes, I think twenty is better."

After much umming and ahhring, we finally agreed on twenty four a square metre and we would pay his tax and a topographic survey of the land, to be deducted from the final price.

The next day there was another knock at the door.

"*Yia sou*, Michali. You have problem, but I make it go away if you pay deposit."

Apparently, not all the olive trees on the land were owned by Manolis. Four were owned by other people! He wanted money to buy the trees and it was to come off the total payment. We instructed our lawyer to make the necessary arrangements.

The big day finally arrived. We assembled at the local notary's office for the reading of the contract. We sat down, conscious of our bulging INKA bags stuffed with loads of dosh.

The notary sat at his desk. Looking up and peering over half moon glasses, he bid us good morning and with a deep sigh leant back in his chair and commenced to read through the contract in a measured voice. Page after boring page was gone through, covering every minute detail of the buyers' and sellers' respective families and who owned what on each of the land boundaries. As if vultures looking for a quick snack, the lawyers clawed at the topographic, pouring over every detail. Half an hour crawled by until we got to the point of handing over the cash. One lawyer entered figures into a calculator. The other agreed the final sum. I began counting out the cash.

"This is wrong!"

Everyone stared. How could it be? The figures had all been checked but this was three times more than we had agreed! So much for the smooth transition of national currencies into euros. I had been calculating in euros, and Manolis was still working in thousands of drachmas!

However, a few days later we did agree a price and we are now proud landowners.

Farewell, Stefane

Village social occasions always seem to revolve around

name days, weddings and funerals.

It is easy to become all pilaffed out from the number of weddings we are invited to. Hours are spent trying to park somewhere near the church, more hours in a jam attempting to drive away, further time sitting at tables waiting for the happy couple to arrive and then copious feasts, requiring the devouring of endless mountains of food and quaffing lakes of wine. You can, therefore, appreciate that late nights, or should I say early mornings, are beginning to take their toll. Many local people we know have more than twenty weddings to go to each year. How do they stand the pace?

Having returned from the last one in the wee small hours, we had a lie in. Much to the chickens' chagrin, I was late with their feed and got a pecking off from the rooster. Pauline was in the shower when the call came through.

"Stefanos, he died. He is buried this morning, but we don't know if he be at the church!"

It took a few moments to translate this cryptic message. Apparently, Stefanos had died in Athens the previous evening, and it was touch and go whether he was going to make the ferry, and, if he did, could it sail because the sea was rough?

We dutifully arrived at the village church expecting a sombre occasion, but everyone was chatting and smiling. In line with everyone else we bought a brown coloured candle. Was Stefanos here? We didn't like to ask - it seemed unseemly. If he wasn't, could the hearse at this very moment be on its way, storming up the mountain with its silent passenger? I looked around; nobody appeared to be going into the church, but we could hear the Papas chanting inside. And then I got confirmation that all was well. Stefanos was in the house. There, parked between two mopeds, stood the coffin lid!

More people arrived and the chatting crowd outside grew and spilled out of the shaded courtyard into the bright sunshine and the graveyard across the lane.

We saw Andonis and Rula and stood with them. Not one to beat about the bush Andonis immediately asked whether we knew what Stefanos had died of. We shook our heads. Andonis put himself about and came back with the answer moments later.

"He died from the kidneys!"

I didn't like to ask whether it had been failure or something he'd eaten.

A white haired old man approached us, looking very worried. He drew Andonis away and whispered something. Andonis looked to the heavens, shrugged his shoulders and nodded. A moment later I saw him drive away in his truck, only to see him return five minutes later carrying a bag of tools.

A funeral is obviously a social occasion where friends and relatives catch up with the latest gossip. As we chatted with Rula, in the corner of my eye I caught what seemed like a demented Andonis swinging a club hammer amongst all the marble headstones. He was smashing something in the graveyard! Rula appeared surprised and turned to ask someone, who shook her head but passed on the enquiry. In moments the Chinese whispers returned with the message that Stefanos' nearest and dearest had all been short, and the family mausoleum had, therefore, been built accordingly. Unfortunately, nobody had stopped to consider that Stefanos was a big man in height and girth and was unlikely to fit!

By now Andonis was in a sweat working against the clock. It would be too upsetting for Stefanos to arrive at his resting place, without being able to go in. We could hear the crash of broken stone and an instruction being barked. Andonis dashed in from the graveyard and grabbed the coffin lid. Lifting it on his shoulder, he turned to speak to someone, causing an old man and his wife to move faster than they had moved in many a long year. As the lid whipped round, they ducked. If it had made contact, there would have been two additional funerals!

Andonis obviously wanted the casket lid to check for fit. Thankfully, it did and Stefanos went to the family vault a happy man without further earthly hindrance.

The olive chainsaw massacre

Another busy time in the village is olive picking from November through to January. Life as an olive farmer can be extremely arduous. As a gentleman farmer, I did think about hiring a couple of Albanians or Bulgarians - or anyone really - but everyone had been snapped up by locals. In the end, we plumped for two English virgins. Not in the biblical sense you understand, but purely by way of experience in the olive picking department.

Derek and Sylvia are 'pensioners', insofar as they support a decrepit UK football team called Chelsea.

"Now here's the score," I told them. "We don't have any fancy flailing equipment; we pick the olives in the traditional way, with the normal deal. You don't get paid - you receive half the oil."

We covered the ground with nylon matting around the first tree and began to smack the living daylights out of it. Olives rained down as if there was no tomorrow, sounding as if we were in the midst of a heavy hail storm. Soon the grey sheets were covered in countless berries plus half the tree's foliage.

"There's still a lot up there," I pointed, helpfully.

"Yeah, we'll need a ladder," moaned Derek, sartorially resplendent in track suit, wellingtons and strange tartan cap with a bright red bobble.

I fetched the ladder, and helpfully held it steady. Disgruntled, he climbed up grumbling something about no danger money.

"It's a waste of time. I can't reach anymore," complained Derek, who has one foot in the grave and the same humour as Victor Meldrew.

Blow this for a game of soldiers; it was going to take forever. Half the olives were bouncing off the sheets into no-man's land and Pauline and Sylvia, sorting beneath, were complaining whenever they were hit by a deluge of berries. I looked around. I could hear the high pitched whine of machines all around, but couldn't see anyone. Anyone, that is, who would appear out of nowhere and tell us we shouldn't be doing it like that. We had a lot to do and a few short cuts wouldn't go amiss. I reached for the chainsaw. This was British thinking at its best, pushing tradition forward with new, innovative ideas - well, OK, maybe not innovation but it was definitely a new approach to olive farming.

I handed Derek the chainsaw. I don't do chainsaws.

After several false starts he got it going and gingerly climbed the ladder clutching a happily chugging saw. Each time he reached the top rung the motor would immediately cut out and down he'd come, moaning, to repeat the whole process again and again and again! This pantomime was repeated six times but, at last, the chainsaw massacre began and Derek became lost amidst the canopy of foliage above us. Suddenly, the saw stalled and in the ensuing silence a cry rang out.

"My finger!"

I looked up for a flying digit, but could only see leaves raining down. A mumbling, grumbling Derek descended from on high with a bloodied hand.

"It's only a flesh wound," retorted a sympathetic Sylvia.

"Yeah, but I could have lost my finger," carped Derek.

A hastily applied plaster set matters to right and we were back in action. The raucous buzz of chain saw against wood wrought the air as Derek gave the tree a haircut from hell. In fact, it was more a case of major surgery. Within fifteen minutes one tree trunk was all that was left, severed to chest height. This was my cunning plan - no more olive picking for three years!

With every half tree now floored, the mountain had come to Mohammed. Leisurely we each selected a branch and beat off all the olives - easy peasy. Soon all empty branches had been discarded and we began to bucket up the spoils. This was easier, and much faster than conventional harvesting, if a little drastic. Within thirty minutes we moved on to the next tree to repeat the same process.

I can't understand why our neighbours whinge and complain about being so tired doing their olives with nylon matting. With this advanced harvesting regime our two trees were completed in half a day!

Kalinykta

To celebrate the end of olive picking and our harvest of eight litres of oil, we decided to enjoy the culinary delights of a local taverna. I say "a", because prior to the influx of tourists, they are few and far between. And not only that, it was Monday night and those normally open were closed. Nevertheless, we drove down the mountain and along the coast road seeking a hostelry which was serving food. Eventually, we found one. The place was packed - just us and dozens of huge pot plants ready to go outside for the summer. We studied the menu. There was quite a choice. It was going to take time to decide. A tincture or two was called for.

"Do you have wine? In a bottle, not village wine. A nice dry red?"

The taverna owner nodded and brought over what looked like a respectable bottle of Cabinet Sauvignon.

"I don't know if this is good. A friend, he gave it to me, as a present. If you don't like, I won't charge. If you do like, you can't have any more. He only gave me one."

He poured three glasses, which made a considerable inroad into any opportunity for a top up. Unabashed, he picked up a glass for himself.

"I must try wine to thank my friend. *Yia mas!* Where you from, Germany?"

"No, England."

"You not English. English planes not here until April."

"Yes we are. We live here."

Not believing us for one moment, he gave us the third degree demanding to know which was our village, and who we knew there. In the end he was satisfied, because a friend of a friend of ours happened to be his third cousin.

We looked at the menu and deliberated and finally came to a decision.

Chicken with lemon. No? Rabbit stifado. No?

We went through the menu with second and third choices with the taverna owner shaking his head at every choice.

"I sorry. We wait for the holiday season," he apologised. "You come back. We have everything then."

My stomach couldn't wait that long. In the end, we ordered pork chops. Two minutes later, out in the darkness, we heard the squeal of brakes and saw our host remonstrating with an angry driver over who was the cause of a possible collision. Remembering his mission, the taverna owner cut short his arguing and disappeared into the butchers across the street. Two minutes later, with the speed of an armed robber leaving a bank, he reappeared clutching two huge *brizoles*.

And very nice they were too, except we had no lemons.

"Sorry, sorry!"

With that our intrepid restaurateur again sped out into the darkness. Minutes passed before he came back into vision clasping two lemons against his chest and sucking his hand. He plonked the fruit down on the table.

"Damned lemons. I couldn't see and the tree bite me - look," and he showed us his bleeding thumb!

He peered at our plates. "*Brizoles* good? My cousin killed a pig today. Very good meat from his shop. It still warm. Enjoy your meal."

The food was indeed very good but Pauline has a small appetite - thankfully - because I haven't, and she passed half her meat over to my plate.

Immediately, our Greek Basil Fawlty leapt out from behind a palm, demanding, "You no like my cousin's pig meat? It fresh. Killed today!"

With typical British reserve and stoic refusal to cause any offence, I tried to explain.

"Sorry. It is too much for my wife to eat."

"Why you come here if your wife not hungry?"

"No, we were hungry but my wife has small appetite and the *brizola* was too large."

"You believe my cousin's pig too big? It was young - only six months old!"

Eventually, I got through, the troubled waters were calmed and we were left to continue our meal. Except a minute later we were presented with three huge apples and a bottle of raki.

"I must go now. I have job in morning. Eat. Drink. Next time I spend more time with you. Leave money on table and close door please. *Kalinykta.*"

We savoured the experience and did as we were told.

CHAPTER SIX

Mad dog of an Englishman

I have been having electronic intercourse via the internet with an Englishman. No it's not a chat room but more of a Samaritan help line. I have been corresponding with someone about to jump off into the unknown and move lock stock and barrel to the island.

Four years ago Robin and Sue fell in love with the village and had come up with the idea of opening a hotel with a taverna offering home-cooked English food. And this was how Robin's Nest was born, or hatched.

I might add this has gone down like a lead balloon with my friend Michalis, who believes that all English food is no more than over-boiled vegetables, no salt and far, far worse, no olive oil.

"Who would eat such food," he exclaimed? "Why, even my pigs would refuse it!"

Robin and Sue have invested heavily in having a hotel built with five apartments, pool and taverna. Except it's not quite built yet! There are no tiles laid, doors, or windows and only a hole where the pool is supposed to be.

And then I got an e-mail that said, "The house is sold. We're coming over!"

The entrepreneurial spirit began to burn brighter.

"We're bringing cases of baked beans and lemonade from ASDA. They were on special!"

"We've collected twelve bicycles from the local rubbish tip. I am going to do them up and offer them for rental!" As we

live in a mountain village, I don't really think the idea will
catch on.

"I've met some Page Three girls who have offered to come
over and open the hotel!" Now, I could see some of the old
boys in the village going for that one.

"Help!"

My son-in-law and I were drinking coffee when we heard
the plaintive cry recorded on the answer-machine. Looking
at each other knowingly, we continued to drink in silence.

"The container's arrived then," remarked Shaun.

"Give him half an hour; it's only nine 'o clock."

Robin had been the advance party and now his worst
nightmare had just arrived. He'd done a really good deal in
the UK; a fully packed, forty foot container, shipped, insured
and unpacked at the door, except.....

The container couldn't make it through the village, so
everything had to be ferried down to Robin's Nest, which
stands some four metres above the road, and then brought
up an impossibly angled earth ramp. In addition to that, the
agents had failed to send a gang of helpers - only a sullen
driver who made it quite clear that manhandling of items
from said container was not in his job description.
Consequently, it was down to Robin to empty this vast cavern
on wheels by himself.

A blast on our horn heralded the arrival of the cavalry or,
more aptly, the walking wounded. I have a hernia and Shaun
had just had a minor op, but which he refers to as major
surgery. That said, it was all hands to the pump - that is,
except the driver who had gone off for coffee.

I lost count of the number of cartons we un-loaded and
became immersed in the three dimensional private diary being
carried inside. Why bring a carton of coat hangers? What were
the twelve bicycles and the three Merry Tillers all about? And
the 1984 fax machine which won't work? Were the forty plastic
chairs really cheaper from ASDA? And the ex-railway espresso
machine that was so heavy it took the three of us to carry?

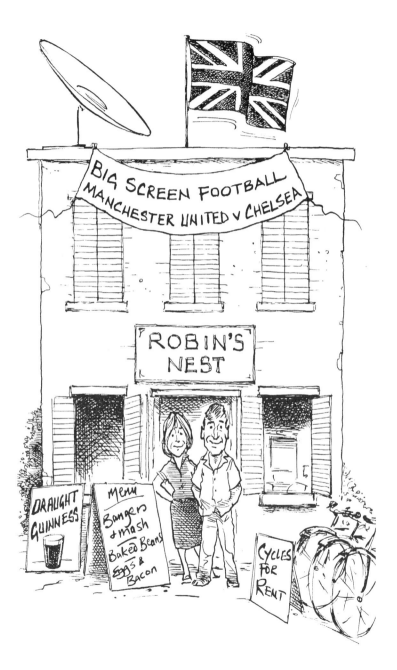

Hour after hour we laboured until a breathless, diminutive figure appeared at the bottom of the ramp.

"Mike, the law has arrived. What do I do?" cried a wheezing Robin?

Apparently, we weren't working quickly enough. The driver had finished his lunch and wanted to get off. He phoned his governor who verified he was now in overtime mode. One hundred euros please. A knackered Robin had apparently told the driver where to go, resulting in the local constabulary being called. The driver didn't understand English, but somehow bad language seems to be an international language!

Robin signed his life away on the promise of paying the sum requested within the next seven days. The matter was resolved. The policeman was happy, the driver was unhappy and Robin was ****** off!

The driver had another 'get off early' strategy up his sleeve. He was leaving in an hour, whether the container had been emptied or not.

The three of us looked into the container. It still seemed half full! We set to and began building a pile of assorted cartons, furniture, washing machine, fridge, table, chairs, cuddly toy, which stretched all along the side of the road. An hour just sped by. It does when you're enjoying yourself!

As if making a point, the driver started the engine. We continued off-loading in a cloud of blue smoke and diesel fumes. It seemed never ending. I looked back. A vast car boot sale disappeared into the distance, where an old lady in black was prodding at a box. She came nearer and shook her head.

"*Polla pragmata!*"

I explained we were working against time, and before I knew what was happening the dear old lady began mucking in. Robin off-loaded a carton, only for it to be grabbed by our new little helper.

"It's heavy," gasped a worried Robin, not understanding her reply.

Loosely translated, she said, "It might be for you, but not

for me!"

At last there was the end of the container and the last item - a bloody motorbike! I was having none of that. I've got a hernia. Super Gran appeared with a scaffolding plank and barked instructions. Gradually the bike was inched down, all half ton of it. Hurrah! The container was empty. A grateful Robin rode home, our lady in black perched side saddle on the motorbike.

Newfangled technology

This week Robin's Nest had the electric wiring completed, although it's still only a building supply, which means they have to juggle all the appliances. There's not enough power to go round, and switching on the electric kettle can cause lights to dim and the computer to crash.

Whilst coping with the unexpected on the building front, Robin and Sue appear to be somewhat daunted by technology. It's not that they are frightened of modern electronics and telephony, in fact they embrace it, but somehow the wrong buttons are pressed and things always seem to go wrong.

Take a simple cell phone. Robin has three. He brought them over from the UK and went through a fortune in phone cards, as if there was no tomorrow, until he discovered that calling the next village meant being routed via the UK.

Although now nearly literate in mobile telephony, Robin invariably forgets to switch his on and Sue forgets to take hers out. This makes communication a mite difficult. Robin has now mastered the art of texting and spends hours laboriously keying in messages. To be fair, where their hotel is built you have to climb up onto the roof and lean over the edge, three stories up, in order to get adequate reception and launch a message into the ether.

Quite often we'll receive a text inviting us to come over for a drink. I don't know why, but messages from Robin, which have to travel all of four hundred metres, seem to go round the world before they arrive with us - two days later. This can make an invitation for dinner somewhat confusing. Was it for last week or next?

The long awaited day of the telephone landline arrived. Notwithstanding delays caused by not having a telegraph pole nearby, the very helpful OTE man tried to short circuit matters by temporarily connecting the telephone into the hotel's wiring for room bells. This did not work, and a further week elapsed before they were connected to the rest of the world.

Thinking answer machines and faxes wouldn't be available in Greece, Robin brought his over from the UK. The fax works fine, except the machine doesn't ring, which makes switching the telephone to fax a bit hit and miss.

They installed the answer-machine. Nobody spoke to Robin and Sue for days. Had they returned to the UK? No. It was simply the machine was set to ring only three times and every time someone called, they had to leave a message because Robin and Sue weren't quick enough running down three flights of hotel stairs to answer the phone.

We then had a tremendous storm. Every time our intrepid duo made a call, no matter what number they dialed, they could only get through to a Greek family. And every time someone phoned Robin and Sue, this same poor family got all their calls.

Getting onto the internet was a little fraught, but Robin managed it in the end. Having now mastered the computer, he was ready for a giant technological step forward. Without satellite TV, they soon worked through their video and DVD collection. We suggested maybe they could get some films copied onto DVD.

I wish to make it quite clear; I do not illegally reproduce material from the television or any other source. A third person was involved, and I made sure that when this illegal process took place, I had a watertight alibi in case we were raided.

Robin prides himself on being a bargain hunter. He turned up with a bag, proudly boasting he had bought DVDs for only thirty cents each. Unfortunately, these weren't DVDs - just the plastic cases.

A few days later he turned up with another bag, exclaiming he'd got it right this time. Proudly he pulled out a full pack of ....CDs!

Technology might be one step for man, but a giant leap for Robin, who also has the habit of leaping without first engaging his brain.

Michalis had just killed six pigs, which were festooned on his veranda, gently swaying in the breeze. Always one for a deal, Robin obviously found these irresistible and ordered a pig quarter and then forgot to think for a moment before telling Michalis he'd love some pig skin for pork scratchings and a head to make brawn.

Robin opened his door the next morning and there on the terrace, gazing up at him, sat six forlorn looking pig heads and enough pig skin to shoe a regiment. There's a lot of meat on a pig's head and, let me tell you, six makes an awful lot of brawn, except.... you need aspic jelly for brawn. But where to get it? The accompanying twenty four pig's trotters were just the ticket. For the whole of the next day Sue had huge vats on the go, boiling the trotters and cooking heads to make traditional English pork pies. The whole scene resembled Sweeny Todd's.

And the pork scratchings?

Robin scratched his head and pondered the problem. All that skin had to be shaved. He devised a cunning plan. Wooden banisters had just been fitted to the staircase and were perfect for draping skins over. He lit a blow torch and set to work. Fortunately, Michalis arrived in the nick of time before Robin could burn the place down. Michalis knew of an even more cunning plan and couldn't understand why Robin was doing what he was doing. Doesn't everyone know you remove pig's hair by dousing the skin with hot water and the bristles then simply scrape off?

A wave of tourists

The first guest is surely due to arrive soon.

In fact, there has been quite a trickle of visitors to the village. This week I found a lone hiker draped over the wall in the lane outside. He had obviously just slogged his way up the mountain. Out of shape, red faced and leaking from every pore, he sported a huge survival back pack, bum-bag, baggy shorts, vest, socks, hiking boots and an Olympic baseball cap worn over a handkerchief.

"*Kalimera*," I called cheerfully. Too exhausted to speak, he limply raised a lifeless arm in response.

Summer has obviously arrived because these various human oddities have been appearing in their ones and twos, as if on a mission to reconnoitre for the expected hordes to come.

It seems as if these advance parties are specialists in particular skills. There are the explorers with their boots and back packs, clutching a map as if it were a dowsing stick, following a yellow brick road to an ancient site located somewhere, anywhere, in the bright blue yonder. "It's on the map, so it must be there," is their maxim, and they won't be budged from this doctrine, despite being told by locals that that cave can only be reached by boat.

Herds of red faced runners are another breed, jogging past as if on a quest, while flocks of cyclists in brightly coloured leotards and pointy helmets swish by downhill, only to return panting and pedalling furiously against the unrelenting incline.

Then there are the legions of more sensitive souls. These can surprise you as they tend to be found behind trees, or large rocks, clutching binoculars, large nets or cameras. However, of late these artistic spirits have become braver, appearing in clusters, oohing and aaghing and pointing to something very important, such as a dot of a bird winging its way above the gorge, which sends the whole group into ecstasies. Demented storm troopers arrive, armed with butterfly nets swooping the air at anything that flies, while the snappers lunge their macro-zooms into the face of an unsuspecting bloom, as if it were endangered flora. The more sedentary of the arty squad squat on tiny stools to sketch and paint.

Once the advance party have been and gone, the hardy "I'm on holiday so I'm going to swim" brigade arrive. Our cove is barely wide enough to pitch a cricket wicket, but every day as many as thirty or so basking tourists are to be found there.

Last week they were all laying there quietly, soaking up the rays or buried in a book. It was peacefully quiet, when from amidst all the prone bodies a lone figure stood up. The bronzed Adonis, wearing only a thong, extended his arms to the heavens as if making an offering to the Gods, and then, obviously feeling somewhat overdressed, calmly removed his excuse for clothing. Elbows nudged, feet kicked and fingers poked awake sleeping members of the silent majority. Minus his fig leaf and as naked as nature intended, Adam strutted his stuff towards the sea. Not a walrus grunted, muttered or moved. The only movement on the beach stemmed from eyes swivelling in their sockets. Only after the two vanilla ice cream scoops of finely honed buttocks had jumped an incoming wave and disappeared beneath the water could there be heard a soft murmuring of complaints wafting away on the breeze.

Moments later, the figure could be seen floating tantalisingly on his back, with extremities displaying a life all their own, wallowing lazily in the warm current like some strange jelly fish in a mass of seaweed.

After several minutes he returned to the beach and I noted the water must obviously still be chilly at this time of year. What nationality could the brazen exhibitionist be? Obviously not English; it wasn't the done thing. Too dark to be Scandinavian. Maybe German?

With his back to the dormant audience, he bent down and

began dressing, pulling on his thong and a tee shirt before striding towards his hired motorbike and roaring off into the sun.

Of course! It was obvious. You could see it in the way he walked. He was French! Definitely frog's legs.

And so the seasons wax and wane, tourists come, tourists go, the incubator shells out chicks on the food chain and I despatch them at the other end. And life in the village continues the way it has done for centuries past, except for one or two changes.

There used to be only one telephone in the village, at the *kafenion*. Roxannie would answer it, step outside and shout out - Yianni! *Tilefono*! - at the top of her voice. The sound would echo round the mountainside, and two minutes later four Yiannises would come running to answer the phone. Now, everyone has a mobile.

But despite technology bringing more material luxuries to the village, the same sense of values remain. Friendship, conviviality and kindness still flourish, as they always did. It is the perfect place to live in the village.

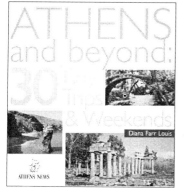

BRIAN CHURCHOPOULOS

Learn Greek in 25 Years,
a crash course for the
linguistically challenged 1999,
reprinted 2000

66 Andy Warhol's famous
prediction that everyone will spend
15 minutes trying to pronounce
ωτορινολαρυγγολόγος (ear, nose and
throat specialist) has already come
true 99